Trouble at Painted River

Outlaw Birch Hamilton was born Birch Kent, a bastard boy who was thrust into a life of crime at the age of sixteen. Now he was attempting to do the near impossible – break out of Yuma Territorial Prison.

Once out, his plans are two-fold: to return home to see his beloved mother and to be reunited with the woman he has loved since his youth. He also intends to settle a score with the meanest man he ever knew – his father. But with bounty hunters and the law on his trail, and his outlaw partner Molly Floyd at his side, Birch's plans prove far from straightforward.

Trouble at Painted River

Matt Cole

A Black Horse Western

ROBERT HALE

© Matt Cole 2018
First published in Great Britain 2018

ISBN 978-0-7198-2625-2

The Crowood Press
The Stable Block
Crowood Lane
Ramsbury
Marlborough
Wiltshire SN8 2HR

www.bhwesterns.com

Robert Hale is an imprint
of The Crowood Press

Where the shimmering sands of the desert beat
In waves to the foot-hills' rugged line,
And cat-claw and cactus and brown mesquite
Elbow the cedar and mountain pine. . . .

Sharlot M. Hall, 'Two Bits', 1902

'Fort Yuma is probably the hottest place on earth.
The thermometer stays at one hundred and twenty
in the shade there all the time – except when it varies
and goes higher. It is a U.S. military post, and its
occupants get so used to the terrific heat that they
suffer without it. There is a tradition... that a very,
very wicked soldier died there, once, and of course,
went straight to the hottest corner of perdition, –
and the next day he telegraphed back for his blan-
kets. '

George Derby, quoted in Mark Twain,
Roughing It, 1872

Land of extremes. Land of contrasts. Land of surprises. Land of contradictions. A land that is never to be fully understood but always to be loved by sons and daughters sprung from such a diversity of origins, animated by such a diversity of motives and ideals, that generations must pass before they can ever fully understand each other. That is Arizona.

Arizona: A State Guide, compiled by Workers of the

Writers' Program of the Work Projects Administration in the State of Arizona, 1940

Arizona is young and daring. She is not tied to precedent, to convention, to other states' ways of doing things. . . . She is bent on making her own ways, and in her own way. Her mistakes will be her own, and her triumphs likewise.

George Wharton James, Arizona, the Wonderland, 1917

Few countries in the world present so marvelous a variety of scenic features as does Arizona . . . the youngest of the American States, and yet one of the oldest lands of the whole continent. . . . What a wonderland of wild cactus growth, of solitude, of mystery, of silence it is! Miles and miles of such weary, cactus-strewn, alkali solitude. . . .

George Wharton James, Arizona, the Wonderland, 1917

CHAPTER 1

YUMA, ARIZONA AT AN UNGODLY HOUR

On July 1, 1876, seven convicts were led up Prison Hill, and placed in their permanent quarters, which they'd helped build. Construction had not yet been completed, so work by the convicts continued. Constructed with smoothly-plastered walls painted with whitewash, enhanced the beauty of this center of learning. With the coming of electrical power, large blowers were installed to help circulate the hot air that hung within the main cell block. Yuma Territorial Prison was created.

Yuma was put on the map for Americans with the gold rush of 1849, when thousands of fortune hunters headed west, seeking the quickest way to reach California.

Most residents of Yuma had no such convenience

– but they did have their freedom. With these 'luxuries', including the prison hospital, the Territorial Prison at Yuma was considered 'state of the art', one of the finest prisons in America.

Although townsfolk were wont to refer to the prison as 'the hotel' and sometimes complained that the inmates were pampered, life there was no picnic.

Many inmates learned to read and write at the prison, which held a good library. They also received regular medical care and ate a filling, if somewhat monotonous diet – heavy on bacon, beans and bread, but often supplemented with rice, fruit, potatoes and beef.

However, the prison was filled with bedbugs, cockroaches, black widows and the occasional scorpion, and life inside was difficult, as it would have been in any penitentiary at that time. When prisoners first arrived, they were questioned as to their nationality, education, occupation and religion. Their heads were shaved and their pictures taken. They bathed and were issued uniforms of alternate black-gray or black-yellow stripes that ran vertically or horizontally. When the prisoners entered the prison, they were allowed to have a cap, two pairs of underwear, two handkerchiefs, two towels, one extra pair of pants, two pairs of socks and one pair of shoes. Officials permitted prisoners to have a toothbrush, comb, photographs, a toothpick, books, tobacco and bedding.

And prisoners knew that if they acted up, guards would strip them to their underwear and chain them inside the dreaded 'Dark Cell', a five-foot-high iron cage set in the middle of a room that had been carved into solid rock. The 'hole' was where prisoners restricted to solitary confinement ended up. Usually one stay would correct even the most incorrigible prisoner's attitude as he or she sat in the pitch-black hole, and was fed bread and water a couple of times a day.

Over the next few days, those wayward prisoners could contemplate their misdeeds with few distractions – there was no bed in the Dark Cell and no sanitation facilities. The only light filtered through a small ventilation tunnel in the ceiling.

The blue jacket was far too tight, for Yuma Territorial Prison inmate #1871 Birch Hamilton had the deepest chest in the prison. But he held his breath and got it buttoned before donning the guard's billed cap. It was a large size and just fitted over the convict's close-cropped red thatch of hair. The guard offered no protest as his black calf boots were removed; he was lying unconscious on the cold stone floor. The prison had more modern amenities than most homes in Yuma, like electricity, forced ventilation, sanitation, including two bathtubs and three showers and a library with two thousand or so books; the most in the Arizona Territory at the time. Yet, prisoners feared and loathed the territorial prison. They said it had insufferable heat . . . that made the place an inferno. It was surrounded in all directions by either rivers, quicksand or desert. It also had an inhuman 'Snake Den' and Ball and Chain as standard punishment. And they said it was impossible to endure, more impossible to escape – or so they thought.

Birch Hamilton did not think that was the case.

The only sound in the long passageway now was that of Birch's breathing as he checked out the gun that had been smuggled to him that day inside a hollowed-out Bible – thank the Lord – by the 'Prisoner's Angel', Miss Letha Blount, known only to Birch as Molly Floyd – his mistress of the owl hoot trail. A snug, little two-shot derringer, it was useless at a distance, but lethal at close range. It had proven good enough to force Guard Jones to release him from his cell, and now it would either get him all the way out, or into an early grave.

For nearly five years he had been in the territorial prison and that had been long enough, in fact, it had been too long for Birch Hamilton alias Kent.

It would be tonight or not ever.

The two blue-uniformed guards stationed in his section of the prison were smoking cigarettes and sipping coffee when trouble with a capital 'T' suddenly appeared on the opposite side of the barrel gate: Birch Hamilton with a gun. Just the sudden sight of the rugged prisoner, free of his cell and staring at them through the bars in the middle of the night would have been enough, but the added fact that he was presently armed was sufficient to make their hearts skip a beat.

No prison guard carried a gun. It was against

orders. The warden did not want any of his homicidal convict 'guests' overpowering a guard and taking a gun. This was a good system – providing the inmates did not have any weapons of their own.

Prisoner Birch Hamilton had one now.

Birch's voice was rough and deep, made harsh by endless, freezing nights spent in the snake den for breaches ranging from insolence to beating guards senseless with his huge, iron fists.

This was a wild one, maybe the wildest in the territorial prison, perhaps all of Arizona. And he was offering them a choice; unlock the door or die. Not much of one, but still a choice.

While hundreds of other unwitting inmates slept on, dreaming about the freedom that many would never live to see, Birch Hamilton reached out for his own.

'There is two of you sons of bitches, and I have got two bullets in this gun. What is it goin' to be?' Hamilton posed.

The guards did not want to die, of course they didn't, and they believed this man would not hesitate in killing them. The heavy key grated in the lock and Birch Hamilton stepped through into the stone-walled guardroom.

The muzzle of his derringer touched the smaller guard's brow, and the well-oiled click of the hammer cocking was low and menacing. This guard's nickname was 'Blackjack', a tag he had earned because of his over-enthusiastic use of the two-foot-long Billy club with which Yuma Territorial Prison guards

13

maintained discipline. Birch had felt the weight of Blackjack's club more often than he could remember. And right now, Blackjack sweated blood.

Birch Hamilton's left fist suddenly blurred and buried itself in Blackjack's belly, causing him to double over. The derringer rose and fell in a clubbing arc, driving the hunched-over man's face into the floor.

The second guard, as big as a barn, threw a desperate punch. Birch went under it, twisted smoothly from the waist and slammed a left hook into his jaw. As the guard went cross-eyed, a knee whipped into his groin to bring him to his knees, where a kick to the jaw rolled him on to his back.

In the lamplight, Birch's large shadow and figure loomed over the unconscious pair, his chest heaving, and his face alight. It felt so good he could not believe it. He had waited nearly five years for this – retribution or payback, call it what you want – it was worth it.

The sound of a door creaking open and closed somewhere below prompted him to cut short his moment of triumph. He still had a long way to go. Dropping to one knee, he snatched a heavy key ring from the first guard's belt, rose in a smooth, oiled motion and descended the stone stairs to the next level, making no more sound than a flitting, prison shadow.

The solitary guard leaning drowsily against the heavy, rusty door on the next level, never knew what hit him. A short time later, prisoners Ethan Harlan,

Isiah McBride and Winston Lang had been released from their cells as well and were following Birch's stalwart figure along the row towards the guard tower.

Although Birch had tipped off the other members of his work gang that he was breaking out and taking them with him, they had never really believed it. Escape plans were a dime a dozen in tough Yuma Territorial Prison, but nobody ever made it. The last major attempt had left some five or six would-be escapees shot dead and the surviving seventh hanged for his trouble. Since then, escape from Yuma Territorial Prison had been confined to the world of fantasy and make-believe – until tonight.

Tonight was as real as the key ring in one of Birch's big hands and the derringer in the other; as real as the string of unconscious guards in back of him, and now two more were added to that count, as the convicts took a careless pair of sentries by total surprise at the base of the guard tower.

The guard tower led into the south yard, which was fronted by darkened workshops on one side and the stables on the other. The prison cemetery lay to the west as well.

In charge of the stables was a notorious identity of Yuma Territorial Prison, Big Sam. By far the biggest man in the prison, this hulking lifer had, over the years, earned himself the same sort of freedom enjoyed by the guards, until he was now a convict in name only. No longer confined to a cell, he slept in a room in the stables, ate with the guards and was one of the warden's special favorites – a Judas who spied on fellow inmates and supplied endless information about their plots and plans to his superiors.

The last time Birch Hamilton had tried to escape, long before Molly Floyd had come to town to lend him outside assistance, Big Sam was the one who had raised the alarm. Birch had drawn a record ninety days in the snake den for that. No inmate had ever survived even half that time in the awfully hot during the day and bitterly cold at night dungeon.

'Get the horses,' Birch whispered as the bunch entered the dimly lit stables. 'There is something I have got to attend to presently.' He handed Harlan the derringer. 'I won't be needing this.'

He found Big Sam snoring in his over-sized bunk, a grainy photograph of a naked woman tacked to the wall above his head.

Birch stood in the yellow lamplight, savoring the moment. The giant reminded him keenly of someone else he hated even more, and it gave him a twisted kind of thrill to imagine himself rousing that other man out of a deep sleep to face him.

Big Sam's lips fluttered as he exhaled gustily. Fingers touched his face and he brushed at them with a hand the size of a dinner plate. The fingers touched him again, harder. His eyes fluttered open and when he saw the broad-shouldered, uniformed figure standing over him, he threw a half salute and made to rise.

Then recognition hit the prison inmate and

potential escapee. He had heard of some of the previous escape attempts.

'Hamilton?' the massive inmate asked, a little shocked.

'Howdy, Big Boy. I just stopped by to tell you I am escaping again and I thought you might like to spread the word to the whole country, like you did last time,' Birch Hamilton said coldly.

A look of desperate cunning crossed the giant's face when he realized Birch was not armed. He groaned, clasped his head in his arms and rocked to and fro as though ill, then suddenly exploded off the bunk in a savage assault.

Birch Hamilton was waiting impatiently.

He had never hit harder than in that moment as he put arm, shoulder and pivoting body behind a powerhouse right that exploded in the giant's face, crushing his nose and snapping off teeth.

Instantly, Big Sam knew he was seriously hurt. His bloody mouth flew open to shout, but the edge of an iron hand chopped across his throat and almost broke his neck. Birch seized him by the shirtfront and dragged his ruined, terrified face close to his own.

'It is dues-paying time, you yellow Judas dog. Yuma Territorial Prison has lost count of the men you have sent to the hole or the gallows, and in return, you have been given special privileges and given better jobs, softer quarters and even spending money . . . all from the warden. Well, Sam, it is time you got something from the other side. This is from

17

your fellow inmates,' Birch Hamilton said.

Big Sam tried to ward off the next blow, but it was not possible. Always powerful, tonight Birch was fueled by something extra; consuming hatred. Too long suppressed, it now poured forth like molten metal. He felt that had Big Sam been a solid stone wall, he could have punched his way right through him. He settled for the next best thing, his iron-hard blows breaking the giant of a man apart inside before sending him crashing to the floor like a bleeding side of beef.

'I would finish you, scum,' Birch panted, 'only it will be back to the cells for you after tonight, and there is two hundred or more inmates waitin' for you in there. . . .'

When he returned to the stalls, his companions had the horses ready and as they rode across the yard, Birch heard voices. He knew the tower guard was talking to an unexpected visitor who was trying to gain entry – the Prisoner's Angel of hope and beauty.

The man was still leaning over the stone parapet, patiently explaining to the midnight caller why he was unable to admit anyone at this ungodly hour, when Birch's fist clubbed him unconscious.

The alarm was raised when the machinery began to groan and clank and the rusted, iron gates swung wide. But by then, it was already too late. Four hard-ridden horses swept through to join the Prisoner's Angel and the bunch was gone before the first rifle shot echoed across the desert.

Only Birch could have succeeded, the convicts

were saying the next day. And surely only Birch Hamilton would have had the guts to double back and put the torch to the courthouse and the warden's home before making good his escape.

CHAPTER 2

THE MARSHAL AND THE WARDEN

The light-green bonnet was caught in the slipstream of the galloping horses and sucked high into the air before falling away from the riders.

'Goodbye, Miss Letha!' laughed Molly Floyd, tossing her gleaming, raven hair free. The severe figure-restricting black jacket, so familiar to all the lonesome prisoners she had visited over the past half year in Yuma Territorial Prison, was next to go. Underneath, she wore a low-cut blouse of bright-crimson silk. '*Adios*, Prisoner's Angel and hello wild Molly!'

The horsemen at her side yelled in approval, and Isiah McBride beat his mount's rump with his striped prison cap before tossing it away. Then he threw back his head and howled like a curly wolf, the eerie sound floating far and free on the chill, desert wind.

'They said it could not be done and we have done it!' Winston Lang bawled to a ghostly mesquite. 'Hey, Birch, does this feel good or does it feel good?'

Birch could not answer right away, for sentiment was beginning to get to him. Up until now, hate, desperation and violence had been driving him on like a large locomotive charging down a straight stretch of track under full steam. But now, he was choked up with emotion, for even though he had spent the last months reassuring his friends, his woman, and, most importantly, himself, that they would succeed, he had never really completely believed it until this exact moment.

He raised both hands to the stars and managed to get out, 'It is good, Winston boy,' while far behind, the fire glowed and flickered into the night sky. Then he threw back his head and bellowed, 'Yeeehahhh!' and tears ran down the face of the man known as the toughest con in Yuma Territorial Prison

The moon was setting as the escapees stormed over a two mile stretch of sand and mesquite to reach the long range of dunes that marked the start of the real desert. Light-brown, dark-brown, sandstone-brown – every shade of brown, the dunes of the Yuma Desert would be beautiful to any eye, but to these desperate men, they were as lovely as the gates of heaven.

Birch brought his foaming horse alongside Molly's and put his arm around her waist. 'Did my girl do good, or did she do good?' he laughed.

It was no effort for Molly to lean from the saddle and kiss him on the mouth, for she could ride as well as she could shoot, and she shot as well as only a girl reared on the shady side of the law could.

'I did it for you, lover,' she told him, eyes shining, lips as red as a rose. 'My God, Birch, has it really been five years?'

Had it been a long five years since he had had his arm around her slender frame? Yes, it had.

It had been five long years since they had been arrested in Black Canyon City, with Molly drawing a lesser three-year prison term in a county jail, and Birch shipped to Yuma Territorial Prison to begin a life sentence.

Five long years!

But now it felt as though it could have been just yesterday. The moon was as bright, the air as sweet, the feel of her body just as soft and seductive as ever. Maybe more so. Maybe everything was even better than he had imagined it might be, Birch thought as they continued their headlong way towards California or perhaps even Mexico to the south.

This was a sight every inmate would long remember: six guards and a hated trusty all stripped to the waist and lashed to the flogging posts in the Warden's Yard. And the most joyous sight of all was when Sam the trusty's tree-trunk legs gave way and he slumped, crying out in pain as the rawhide thongs bit into his wrists.

The weary warden spoke and a stoic guard strode

across the flagstones to the giant and delivered a ferocious kick. The trusty Sam gasped and somehow hauled himself to his feet. His face was a wreck, a sight that filled every watching convict with delight, for on the hate lists in Yuma Territorial Prison, Trusty Sam was always rated Number One.

It was characteristic of Warden Myron Hurst that, confronted by this major breakout of his administration, he should show more concern for the punishment of those responsible than for the pursuit of the escapees.

Punishment of this nature of prison officials was strictly against the rules set down by the Prison Board, yet, had the entire board shown up at that moment to object personally, it was doubtful if the warden would have been diverted from his purpose. In one night he had lost four inmates, his reputation and his residence. His life was in tatters. Someone had to pay, and until his riders dragged the escapees back, this sorry seven would have to suffice.

'Begin!' he roared, and the floggers moved in to bring cold leather into gruesome union with quivering flesh.

The current residents of Yuma Territorial Prison – the inmates – loved it.

The marshal checked his horse before the blackened remains of the warden's home. The fire had done a thorough job and all that remained of the fine dwelling was an outhouse and an iron water tank. The rest was ashes and twisted metal.

'The Lord works in mysterious ways, Marshal,' the deputy remarked.

'What?' Federal Marshal Rigdon Elliott was studying the footprints in the dust. He did not really expect to find anything of substance or value here, it was just a habit of his. He was a natural hunter, and a good hunter relied on signs the way a sailor relied on the stars.

'Well, I have heard it said that Warden Myron Hurst always lived too high on the hog for a man on his salary. . . .' Marshal Elliott looked up sharply. 'You are not implying that the warden is dishonest are you, Deputy?'

'Oh no, sir,' protested the deputy, even though that was exactly what he was saying.

'Just as well.'

Although Marshal Elliott might be thinking the same way as his deputy, he would not say so, or allow others to do so, unless there was proof to back it up. He was that kind of a lawman: straight, and by the book.

Rigdon Elliott had never had a high regard for the warden of Yuma Territorial Prison, but at the moment, that was the least of his concerns.

Birch Hamilton had escaped Yuma Territorial Prison.

The marshal had the overpowering feeling that before he saw Birch again, either in chains or dead at his feet, a hell of a lot of powder would burn. The smoking ruins of the house and courthouse told the lawman loud and clear what the escapees wanted him

24

to know. They had not just broken out, they had graph-ically illustrated what he could expect from them.

All-out war.

Things were always tense when men who spent their lives hunting down and capturing dangerous outlaws came face to face with those entrusted with their care, who had let them loose again to prey on the world at large. The meeting that took place between Hurst and Elliott a short time later was no different.

The warden was full of excuses among other things, and the marshal had accusations.

'It wasn't my fault, Marshal. I did my best. . . .' the warden pleaded feebly.

'You allowed a *girl* to break out four of the most dangerous men in the territory,' Marshal Elliott fired back.

'That was no ordinary girl, Marshal Elliott.' The warden tried to sound serious.

'Whereas you have proven yourself a *very* ordinary custodian, sir.' The Federal Marshal produced a drawing from a folder. 'Is that the *girl?*'

The wretched prison warden examined the like-ness. It showed a savagely beautiful woman with raven hair and a full mouth. Hurst had to squint and put his imagination to work to envision her in a poke bonnet, spectacles, hair tied back in a severe bun, and dressed from head to toe in sober-gray Quaker cloth. And yet the features were so distinctive that finally, he was able to nod.

'That would be her . . . the one they called the

Prisoner's Angel,' Hurst added.

'Molly Floyd,' Marshal Rigdon Elliott said drily. 'Birch's lover at the time of his arrest in Gila City and released last year after serving a four year stretch in prison herself. You do have a file on Birch, don't you, Warden Hurst?'

The inference was plain. Had the warden been familiar with the files of his inmates, he may have identified the Prisoner's Angel as a bandit, hell raiser and Birch Hamilton's lover.

Warden Hurst's hands shook as he produced the Bible, which he passed across the desk. Opening it, Elliott saw how the pages had been hollowed out in the shape of a derringer. From the moment the Prisoner's Angel had managed to pass the book to Birch without a preliminary examination by the guards, the big escape had been a foregone conclusion.

At that moment, it was possible Federal Marshal Rigdon Elliott was secretly glad the warden's plush house had gone up in flames, even though he would never admit as much.

'He won't be taken alive,' Elliott said, going to the window overlooking the rock quarry.

'How can you be so sure?' the warden snapped in response.

'Because I know the man. Birch isn't like other convicts or other men, Warden Hurst. There is a fire in his belly that nothing can quench.'

'Yes, so I noticed,' Hurst grimaced. 'Tough *hombre*! By glory, I never worked harder to break a man,

Marshal. Three months in the hole once. Three months! And do you know what he was doing when we finally let him out?'

'Tell me.' Marshal Rigdon Elliott had a glare on his face.

The warden looked to be in awe. 'Complaining that the hole was too comfortable. He said if we ever understood how to run a real prison, we would make the hole tough, so characters like himself would not be busting a gut to get thrown in there all the time.'

The marshal's eyes clouded. He knew more about Birch Hamilton than anyone else, although much of this knowledge, for reasons known only to himself, was never made public. For instance, Rigdon Elliott was the only lawman who knew Birch's real name was Kent, not Hamilton.

All the Wanted dodgers would announce the dramatic escape of Birch Hamilton, the outlaw, but the marshal would be searching for Birch Kent.

Maybe that would give him an edge, Elliott reflected. He could sure use one.

'Are you going after him personally, Marshal?' Warden Hurst asked curiously.

'Of course,' Rigdon Elliott fired back, perhaps a little too harshly.

'You say my men won't catch him. I suppose you believe you will?' Hurst tried unsuccessfully to hide a sneer.

'No,' Elliott said. 'I will catch him.' The marshal turned to go. 'And when I return him to prison, Warden Hurst, I will make it my business to see that

27

it is no longer yours.'

Rigdon Elliott found some small satisfaction in that parting shot, but it did not sustain him very long. The reality was bleak. The West was wide open, and Birch Hamilton was an outlaw of uncommon power and determination – and he burned with a hate that made him doubly dangerous.

The task ahead was not going to be easy, and Elliott had no intention of attempting to chase the fast-running hellions around the deserts and prairies. He doubted he would ever get near them that way. Instead, he planned to use his special knowledge of Birch Hamilton to his full advantage. He had a hunch he knew where the man might go.

CHAPTER 3

MONEY AND BLOOD

All around them the desert stretched, vast, mysterious and silent under a sea of stars. The circle around the sound had set all day long, implanting its image against the turquoise blue Arizona sky. Standing on a red knoll above the campsite, Birch drew in a deep breath of cold air and was thrilled by the heady sensation of freedom he was experiencing

Everything was beckoning to him: the wide-open spaces, the unknown, the future. No more stone walls or steel bars. No more stints in the hole, or the stinging touch of the lash. No more lousy jailhouse chow, or the eternal stink of stale cabbage floating up through the levels. From now on, it would be space, speed and freedom for Birch Kent.

Excitement beckoned to him from the dark and gloom. He was rushing headlong to meet it. They had ridden since sun-up over broad mesas, down and

29

out of deep canyons, along the base of the mountain in the wildest parts of the territory. Storms in the dry counties were infrequent, but heavy; and this surely meant a storm was coming to some part of Arizona. Birch hoped to avoid it but secretly hoped the storms would wash away any signs of their tracks.

That night he slept with Molly beneath the great expanse of the sky. The stars were huge and bright; he was certain they had never been like this in all his years in prison. The wind softly sifted the sand and Molly's sleeping face was beautiful in the eerie blue light. Birch lay listening to the muted sounds of jingling harness on the hobbled horses, and fell into a deep sleep as the night wrapped itself protectively around them all – five prison escapees with the bit of freedom between their teeth.

Birch was first to wake. No watch had been set way out here in the desolate heart of nowhere. He rose without disturbing Molly and filled his lungs with the pure air he could never get enough of.

He ran his hands over his chest as he turned to face the east. His vee shaped torso and slender waist were inherited, along with the color of his hair and the timbre of his voice. His face darkened at the thought of Big Sam Eaton and his back began to itch the way it always did whenever his father occupied his thoughts.

Dawn began as a long pale line above the dun colored clouds to the east. The line slowly lengthened and turned red. Then the sunlight was spilling across the desert faster than a horse could gallop.

Molly rose and came to his side.

'These are the times I dreamed of when we were apart, Birch,' Molly said lovingly.

'Me too,' Birch replied caringly.

'Did you ever think you might die in that wretched place?' she asked, suppressing a shiver that the thought gave her.

Birch Hamilton calmly shook his head. 'Never. I wasn't meant to die like some nobody.'

She looked him in the eyes and responded, 'How then?'

The outlaw shrugged. He did not really know how. And this was too good a moment to worry about it at all. Right then, Birch Hamilton – Kent – had never felt more completely alive. He put his arm around Molly's shoulders and they stood thus while the burnished orb of the sun came surging over the horizon to start the new day – the day that would see them reach the town of Socatoon Station, where they boasted a nice, fat bank just waiting for a man like Birch.

The Socatoon Station Cattlemen's Bank was Ethan Harlan's idea. He had been there once or twice, before getting thrown into prison for five years, and had been impressed by the size of the bank and the inadequacy of the law force there, comprising one fat, apparently lazy, sheriff, a skinny scared-looking deputy and a dog – a mutt – employed by the peace officers for tracking down chicken thieves.

The five outlaws, once awake, pressed on towards the town. They dropped into a low, broad watercourse, ascended its bed to big cottonwoods and

31

flowing water, and followed it into box canyons between rim-rock carved fantastically and painted like a Moorish facade. At last, in a widening below a rounded hill, they came upon an adobe house, a fruit tree, and round shaped corral. This was the town of Socatoon Station.

Harlan was pleased to see that things looked pretty much as he remembered. 'Like taking candy from the mouth of babes, *mi amigos,*' he assured the group and Birch, in particular, as they rode in. 'They should rename this place Lazytown or something.'

Birch agreed that Socatoon Station looked harmless and innocent enough. There were men dozing in porch rockers and plump matrons on the timber boardwalks. A kid with a stick batted a ball against the jailhouse wall. The smoke issuing from the jailhouse window carried the aroma of fresh coffee.

The Socatoon Station Cattlemen's Bank stood on a corner ahead. It was a handsome, solid building with a slate roof and gleaming colonial windows covered by discreet iron bars.

'They say,' Molly remarked as they rode past the bank without displaying any interest, 'that the easy looking ones are always the toughest.'

'I like 'em tough,' Birch replied. He was not bragging. The penned-up years in Yuma Territorial Prison had left him hungry – hungry for action, for danger, for striking back, for getting square. As far as he was concerned, the tougher they came, the harder they were bound to fall. The caged beast was on the loose once again.

As they swung in to the saloon hitch rail, Birch saw a woman on the walk. She was in her late forties, still handsome and stately in a flowered, cotton dress and bonnet.

He stared. She reminded him of his dear mother.

Molly said, 'Get your eyes off the ladies, Romeo. I didn't spring you so you could start flirting with anything you see in a skirt.'

Birch laughed as he swung down off his horse; a forced laugh. 'Heck, she is old enough to be my. . . .' He broke off and pushed his hat lower over his eyes as he watched his henchmen dismount. He was all business again as he led the way up the well-worn steps. The woman was gone. He refused to think of his mother as he pushed his way through the batwings and led the way in.

'Bartender,' he hollered, a little bit of drool flicking from his thirsty mouth. 'Five cold ones. Pronto!'

Ethan Harlan, Winston Lang, and Isiah McBride all frowned, not liking the way he was attracting attention. But Birch knew what he was doing. Experience had taught him that the surest way to attract attention was to skulk about trying not to draw attention to yourself.

A fat man wearing a grimy, white apron brought the tray of drinks to their table, and Birch paid him with a silver dollar.

'Hot day,' he commented as he lifted his beer glass.

'They are all that way.' The man ran his right sleeve across his brow, looking the five strangers over.

His eyes lingered on Molly. 'Come across the desert, did you?' They nodded cautiously and the bartender continued. 'Rough for a lady, ain't it?'

'We breed 'em tough in Texas, the ladies too,' Birch said with a toothy grin.

The bartender gave a brief look of surprise. 'Oh, you're from the Lone Star state, then?'

'Yeah. From Texas headin' for California and our share of the gold,' Birch supplied the man.

The man smiled wryly as he moved off. 'Well, best of luck. Reckon you will need it.'

'Not luck,' scar-faced Harlan said softly, his top lip lined with white beer-froth. 'Guts, partner.'

'And greed,' drawled Winston Lang. 'Don't forget greed.'

Isiah McBride hoisted his glass. 'To guts, greed, and tin-pot banks.'

The five outlaws drank together and Birch felt a surge of excitement. This was more like it. This was living. Things were moving and he was making them move.

'Let's get on with it,' he said quietly, draining his glass. 'Suddenly I am feeling pretty damn lucky.'

'We will always be lucky from here on, darlin',' Molly assured him, squeezing his arm. 'This time tomorrow we will be rich, taking it easy at Uncle Claud's across the border.'

Molly Floyd was one of those people who had kinfolk just about everywhere you could think of. She seemed able to produce uncles, aunts, cousins, grandparents, nephews and nieces almost at will.

34

Uncle Claud's sounded fine to Birch. He could rest up a bit there and bask in his new freedom before doing what he must do. . . .

The Socatoon Station Cattlemen's Bank was quiet. A white-haired gentleman chewed the end of his pen at the wooden writing desk. The door of the manager's office stood open and the outlaws could see him leaning back in a comfortable chair chatting to a customer. Two tellers in stiff, celluloid collars manned their cages diligently, blissfully ignorant of their surroundings. There were two clerks in back, poring over thick ledgers.

This was going to be easy, a pushover, the outlaws thought.

Well, almost. . . .

They were halfway through an uncomplicated holdup with staff and customers lined up, frozen, under naked guns, while Lang stuffed money into a canvas sack in the thick-doored vault, when the armed guard sauntered in, whistling an operatic aria.

They had not known about the armed guard.

More importantly, he had not known about them.

The guard, who had been stationed at the bank for nearly six months now without encountering one solitary incident that could be even remotely construed as trouble, had just paid a visit to the water tap in the back room. He was trying to stave off boredom, but that ceased to be a problem when Harlan pivoted away from the line-up and bellowed, 'Put your hands up!'

The guard looked up and started to shout as he clawed for his gun.

'Stupid fool! Always one that wants to be a hero!' Birch snorted in disgust as he leapt forward, gun sweeping in a wide arc. Hard steel made violent contact with a thick skull and the guard was chopped off in mid-holler as he spun in a half circle and broke a table on his ungraceful, noisy fall to the floor.

'Judas Priest!' gasped McBride, darting to the windows. 'Looks like everyone in town heard him. Better get moving, Birch.'

Birch was already making for the door with Molly. As they burst on to the porch, a skinny man wearing a polka dotted shirt and clutching a repeating rifle, came charging towards them from across the street. Not only had everyone heard the guard's roof-lifting bellow, but they had also heard what he had said.

'Bandits in the bank! We are bein' robbed!'

It was exactly the sort of thing designed to have a galvanizing effect on a sleepy little town with a big, fat bank. The townsfolk were coming out of the woodwork like termites on a disturbed mound.

Birch's gun smoked and the man with the spotted shirt stood frozen in terror as his rifle spun in the air with a splintered stock. Two more bullets kicking up dust between his feet from Birch's smoking .45 sent him hopping away in giant, ungainly leaps, while five desperadoes streaked to their horses and hit leather.

The guns began to roar as they stormed down the street. A towner lurched off the walk, clutching his leg and the street quickly filled with gun smoke.

They were almost out of range when Winston Lang stopped the slug that made all the difference and tumbled dead from his racing horse.

Winston Lang had been the one carrying all the money.

CHAPTER 4

LOVE, HATE AND THE LIKE

'Rushin'!' Claud Woodward said in a voice like gravel rolling over a corrugated iron roof. 'That is what you young'uns are doin' rushin' towards the grim hand of death.'

'Well, that is something nobody can say about you, Uncle Claud,' laughed Molly. 'You haven't moved out of a slow crawl in what . . . over a hundred years now, have you?'

'Laugh if you will,' the hawk-faced old man with a long white beard and hair said. 'But you ain't been free a week and there is one less of you already. At that rate, you will all be pushin' up daisies in a month. No loss, you might say, but what about my niece? You cowboys are a dime a dozen, but my Molly's something special.'

They were drinking rye whiskey in the old timer's Proverb Town home, and rapidly getting drunk.

The timeworn man was one of the characteristic 'long hairs'. He had come to the Galiuro Mountains in '70, and since '71 he had lingered there, in spite of man or the angel of death.

Maybe they were grieving some over hard-luck Winston Lang, but the really sad part was losing all the money. . . .

The Socatoon Station job had grossed not one red cent, so what else was there to do, but drink and get drunk?

'You always were an old flatterer, Claud,' smiled Molly, radiant in a red silk shirt and tailored riding pants. 'But I like it.' She sipped her drink. 'How safe are we here?'

'As a bank,' Uncle Claud winked. 'Well, most banks, mebbe. That is if you mean to stay. . . .'

'Don't you want us to?' Molly asked sharply.

'Sure I do,' her uncle insisted.

Claud Woodward had ridden the owl hoot trails in his youth and still regarded himself as a member of the 'dark brotherhood'. It was a wild family, the Woodwards and Floyds, a reckless, close knit and prolific clan spread across two territories and held together by deeply rooted loyalties and a common hostility towards law and order.

Having met Claud Woodward, Birch found himself better able to understand Molly, who was certainly the most remarkable woman he had ever met.

He studied her proudly. She was just like him, or

at least, like the man he would become. Earlier, when he was just a boy, there had been another girl, vastly different from raven-haired Molly. And Birch Kent had been a very different young man from the outlaw, jail breaker and hell raiser he would become.

He realized Uncle Claud was explaining what he meant by their staying on. There was a family reunion about to take place over in Cactus Creek, he revealed, and all the Floyds, Woodwards and more were invited to bring along their friends and as much liquor as they could carry. Uncle Claud planned on going, but only if Molly and her friends went with him, otherwise they would all remain in Proverb Town.

Molly looked a question at Birch, who smiled. 'Sure,' he said. 'Why not? We might be poor, but there is no need for us to be dull and boring to boot.' Then he sobered. 'What is the law situation over there, Claud? They will have dodgers out on us, for certain by now, you know.'

'You don't reckon the Floyds or Woodwards would hold a get together anyplace within fifty miles of a jailhouse, do you, boy?' Uncle Claud snorted, and that was that. They were going to Cactus Creek.

That night, Birch walked the street of Proverb Town alone under a gibbous moon. He did not think about boyish Winston Lang. Life was cheap, whether it be inside or on the dodge. They were treading dangerous pathways wherever they went. There could be a hundred-man posse bristling with guns creeping up on Proverb Town right at that moment, which meant

40

his own life could be over before long. If that was true, he hoped to go out the way Winston Lang had, with a gun in his hand and doing battle with his enemies. But until that moment came, Birch Kent would squeeze every ounce he could out of life and, with luck, do just a couple of the things he wanted to before he died.

He liked the thought of being part of a big family reunion at Cactus Creek.

It would relax him before he traveled south to visit his mother.

A yellowish, mangy looking dog sleeping on the saloon porch let out a sharp yelp of protest as Birch accidentally stepped on its tail.

'Sorry, you mangy mutt, I was miles away,' he said, bending to pat its head and grinning when it licked his hand in return.

He was sober again when he pushed into the musty little saloon. Thinking of Adeline always brought back the pain – not physical pain, but the emotional pain of not having seen her for so long. At times like this, Birch Kent felt like the original loner, who, despite all the people he knew and liked, was only really close to one person and that was his mother.

'What about Andrea?' his inner voice queried.

He ignored it and held up two fingers to the funereal bartender. Two fingers of rye whiskey might not erase a girl named Andrea completely from his mind, but it was a start. 'You have got a girl, Birch,' he muttered into his drink. 'And you have got your freedom. So, don't start getting greedy or stupid.'

As he lowered his glass, he saw a drinker studying him curiously. 'Don't I know you, stranger?'

'Marshal Rigdon Elliott out of Cave Creek,' Birch said brusquely. 'Currently hunting those bloody-handed jail breakers from Yuma Territorial Prison, at your service, sir. I doubt very much that we have met.' He studied the man closely. 'Unless, of course, you have been inside?'

The man suddenly found he had pressing business elsewhere.

Birch grinned as he leaned against the bar, his rugged face flushed with good humor. It was getting better all the time, this heady, intoxicating thing called liberation. He swore they would never again take him alive. There would be no more cages for Birch Hamilton or Birch Kent, whatever name he went by, and that was an invigorating thing to know, even if the alternative to the cage might well be the grave.

But even that thought could not depress him tonight as he stood there feeling the freedom- generated power surging through his body.

He envisioned them hunting him throughout the West; the lawmen, bounty hunters, the army and the rest. The name of Birch Hamilton/Kent would be on every tongue, and they would take heart that one escapee was already dead. They would expect to get him before too long, he suspected, but it was exciting to know they never would.

He drank deeply, and for some reason, the

whiskey was the best he had ever tasted.

He was drinking to the mother he loved and the father he hated.

It was the purest chance that brought Ted Mcleod and Jude Decker to the trail house on the Cactus Creek road the following night.

The two bounty hunters who rode for Naylor were supposed to be combing the desert fringes for signs of the Yuma Territorial Prison fugitives, but a combination of weariness and powerful thirsts had made them head for the trail house.

At the livery in back of the building, big Jude noticed a horse with an uncommon brand, a double Y. Only a bounty hunter would have known, this far from the Yuma Territorial Prison, that it was the brand of the penitentiary horses.

The liveryman told him he had traded this very good horse for a very ordinary one with a man he described as a 'Mex lookin' jasper, who might be the first bald Mexican he had ever seen.'

When Ted and Jude considered that the trade had taken place at night in poor light, they realized that a close-cropped convict haircut could make a man appear to be bald.

They concealed their excitement as they casually asked which trail this bald Mexican had taken.

'Headed for Cactus Creek,' the man simply supplied. 'Seems there is a hell of a lot of folks headin' out there right now. God alone knows why, on account that is some of the most useless country on the plains, even if it is right purty at this time of year.'

Ted and Jude rolled their eyes eloquently at each other as they quit the livery. They made record time riding out to the Gila River camp to report to Naylor.

Naylor was a man who would have cheerfully brought his own mother in, dead or alive, had there been a halfway decent price on her head.

It took a great deal of trial, error and some truly spectacular falls before the Floyd and Woodward menfolk were prepared to concede that the only man present capable of riding a horse at a lope while doing a headstand on a saddle, was Birch.

'Is that what they teach in the United States penal system these days?' a chuckling Uncle Claud enquired. Being the only man there to have sized up Birch before they had arrived at Cactus Creek. Uncle Claud was also the only one to have wagered on him, and he had cleaned up big.

Nobody resented Birch's win. Quite the contrary. Among the score of men, women and children gathered on a round, green knoll beneath the spreading oak trees that gave part of the town some shade, he was a hero.

Of Kentucky hill stock, Molly's kinfolk were born rebels and taught to defy the law. There may have been few full-time outlaws amongst the Floyds and Woodwards, but from the oldest graybeard down to the youngest toddler, there was no love for authority, and only admiration for those who thumbed their noses at it in such a spectacularly successful fashion.

'They like you, Birch,' Molly smiled as, arm in arm, they strolled away from the others and headed for where the food was laid-out on trestles. 'I just knew they would have to – especially the females.'

'Oh, sure. It is the ones under six and over sixty who really take a shine to me, but I don't stand a chance with anybody in between,' he joked.

He halted to pat a child's curly head. She was eating a toffee apple. He had not touched a child or seen a toffee apple in over five years. Sometimes, in retrospect, those long years seemed a lot longer.

'Don't give me that baloney,' Molly said as they moved on. 'All women take a shine to you, mister, and you know it.'

He shrugged. 'You are wrong.'

'Well,' she said, enumerating on her fingers, 'Cousin Emily said you were cute, Aunt Lydia thinks you are quite dashing, while Gramma Floyd, who really should have more to occupy her mind, thinks you have a great body.'

'You are just making that stuff up. Anyway, you know there is only ever been one woman for me, so why are you carrying on?' Birch replied.

'Aren't you forgettin' her?' Molly said.

Birch glanced away. Ever since they had been together, Molly's feminine intuition had been working overtime. She claimed there had been a great love in his life, that he had been hurt, that he was still in love, and he would always love 'her' more than he did her.

'She doesn't exist,' he lied, too easily. 'I thought

45

you would have forgotten about that hog's swill these past five years.'

'Why should I? You certainly haven't forgotten her. Last night, when we made love, I could tell you were thinking of. . . .' she started.

He seized her by both shoulders and shook her. 'Don't go too far, baby.'

Molly laughed. The point of the whole exercise had been to score a reaction. Having succeeded, she was satisfied. Her reason? No woman had ever needed a reason for doing anything.

'Kiss me,' she said. He did and she was happy. They strolled on, guided by the heady scents of roast chicken and buttered corn, to the covered tables.

Cactus Creek was one of the prettiest places Birch had ever seen, a hidden hinterland surrounded by rounded hills where prairie and mountains met. The grass, which Uncle Claud claimed was sour and of no value to stock, was deep green and lush, even in the hot seasons, while fields of blue bonnets nodded their heads in the meadows and on the gently sloping hillsides.

The town comprised a dozen or so houses and a saloon. There was no railroad, telegraph office, jail-house or any of the bothersome burdens of civilization. A slow flowing river circled the town and formed a willow lined backwater where the clan was enjoying its picnic.

This, thought Birch Kent, was about as sharp a contrast to the harsh stone, steel and dust of prison life as a man could possibly find.

Something stirred in the willows. . . .

Afterwards, Birch would castigate himself for not being more alert. But the golden day was seductive, the atmosphere so calm and reassuring that it was easy to believe no evil existed in the whole wide world, and even if it did, there was less of it here than anyplace else.

Ethan Harlan and Isiah McBride were already wolfing down the food in the company of a trio of laughing cousins, while a motherly woman heaped food onto plates for Birch and Molly.

Birch forked a fragrant chunk of fried chicken into his mouth and as he chewed it, gazed off into the distance.

'When?' Molly asked quietly.

'Huh?' he replied immediately.

'When are you planning to leave me?' she said coolly.

He stared at her. 'Leave you? What are you talking about?'

Molly ate neatly and daintily. For a woman who could shoot, ride and fight like a man, she was intensely feminine. She seemed merely curious, but not annoyed, as she went on. 'You have got that look in your eyes, Birch – the faraway look. I know you are thinking of going and I also know you won't tell me where. But I would like to know when.'

Birch washed down the chicken with some passable home-brewed cider then sat cross legged, soaking up the sunshine.

Molly was right, of course. Nobody knew him

better than she did, in the old days had sometimes known what he was thinking about before he was really sure of it himself.

'Tomorrow,' he said finally.

'How long will you be gone?'

He replied directly. 'As long as it takes.'

It sounded rude, but wasn't. He did not know how long. He wasn't even sure if he would be back. There was danger where he was heading, danger in a dozen guises. And the fact that he had to go alone enhanced the danger. He could die.

'Where do you want me to wait?' she asked.

Birch was considering this when he caught the wink of sunlight on something in the shadow of the willows a hundred or so yards away.

His blood ran cold. There was someone in there with a gun.

'Excuse me,' he murmured to Molly, getting to his feet. 'Something I forgot to take care of.'

'Birch!' she called after him, but he was already lengthening his stride as he moved away.

'Heads up!' was all he said to his henchmen, but it was enough. In an instant, Harlan and McBride were following him down the slope.

Molly did not panic when she realized what was happening. Calmly slipping her hand inside her blouse, she touched the pearl handle of the little gun holstered there as she looked around warily. It seemed that everyone except herself was laughing under this golden sun ... innocent, unaware ... perhaps doomed.

Molly walked after her companions who were now rapidly approaching the willows.

A single shot rang out and all hell broke loose.

Birch dived headlong into the tall grass as Harlan and McBride fired a volley of shots into the trees. The ambushers' fire was concentrated on Birch, but because he had moved so fast, the bullets were hitting the ground well behind him as he gained cover of a deadfall.

He drew a bead on a gun flash and fired.

The man who came lurching through the curtain of willow fronds, clutching his midriff, was tall and angular with a gaunt, unshaven face and a broken nose. He was in the act of dropping a Winchester, and two heavy Colts were holstered on his hips.

Birch Kent could almost smell bounty hunter on him.

Picnickers were rushing for cover higher up on the slopes as Birch, Harlan and McBride loosed a thundering volley of fire. But the ambushers answered back in kind and from the corner of his eye, Birch saw McBride falter then fall, sliding on his elbows in the blue bonnets, his face a sudden deathly shade of white.

A bullet parted Birch's hair, and he cursed. They had been careless.

Maybe he had been locked away too long, and had lost his edge!

Ducking low, he reloaded swiftly. From higher up, a revolver roared and he saw that Molly had taken up a position behind a rocky outcrop. What a woman,

Birch mused. And what a pity he could never love her. . . .

He swung to face the willows again. They were using the heavy stuff now. A Big Fifty rifle thundered violently, followed by the blast of a heavy-gauge shotgun.

Lead rattled around the deadfall and Birch decided he had had enough. After firing from one end of the log, he rolled to the other end, bobbed up swiftly and caught a fleeting glimpse of a shadowy figure shifting position. Birch's Colt roared and the ambusher lurched. He fell against a tree, and the noise was deafening as both Harlan and Molly homed on the man, expending lead recklessly, but with deadly accuracy.

Birch grunted in satisfaction as he saw the man slide slowly down the trunk of a tree, leaving a crimson smear behind him, and lie motionless. They were cutting the odds.

'Kent!' a voice bawled out suddenly. 'You can't win this one. Throw down your guns, or we will start in on the women and kids.'

Birch replied with a bullet. Instantly the Big Fifty crashed and behind him he heard somebody scream as lead howled close. That was the last straw.

Seething with white-hot anger and just a little crazy, Birch bounded to his feet and began to run.

Molly screamed at him to get down and the ambushers were shouting in astonishment. But before they could recover and start shooting, Birch was veering off at a tangent, racing across the slope in a low crouch as though making for a gully wash that ran down to the river. Then he changed direction and doubled back to the left as the ambushers' bullets kicked up dirt on the right. While they were adjusting their aim, he straightened up and charged straight for the willows, diving to the ground when he got within ten yards of his goal, then flipping and rolling beneath bursts of gunfire to reach the cool, green shade unscathed.

Fifty paces away, Naylor the bounty hunter paused with his mouth hanging open, to reflect on all the tales he had heard about Birch Kent (Hamilton), and particularly the warnings he had received about how difficult and dangerous it might be to claim his scalp. Birch's courage and lightning speed left the man breathless, but only for a moment. Naylor, too, was a veteran of dangerous situations, just like the man he hunted this day.

'Pour it on, boys,' he roared. 'We got him right where we want him.'

With two of their number lying among the willow leaves, the surviving bounty hunters concentrated their fire on the spot where Birch had disappeared. Here, a recent flood had piled logs, dead vegetation and silt into a pile extending several feet up the gnarled trunk of an old willow tree. Splinters, dust and dead leaves filled the air as the bullets slammed home, and the old willow shook like an octogenarian with the ague.

And the man they were after belly wriggled beneath the veil of dust and gun smoke towards

Naylor's position.

During his headlong charge for the trees, Birch had glimpsed a dry channel running from the old willow tree and parallel to the river. It afforded perfect cover for him now, but his companions did not know it. They thought he had gone crazy and was either already dead or about to die – unless they did something about the situation.

Molly poured in steady covering fire as Harlan got to his feet and charged.

It was the sight of Ethan Harlan streaking down-slope that prompted big Naylor to bob up with a Peacemaker .45 in either hand and open up.

It was, in turn, the sight of Naylor – big, gross-bellied, ugly and perfectly outlined against the blue shimmer of the river, that caused Birch to slide to a halt, throw up his .45, and fire.

It did Birch's heart good to see his bullet catch the bounty killer in the right hip, causing his leg to give way and bringing him crashing to earth.

Despite his wound, Naylor was still full of fight as he surged up on to one knee, beefy face contorted with pain and anger, the twin Peacemakers searching for a target.

Birch took aim and shot him between the eyes.

As Naylor convulsed and fell backwards, flailing in his death throes, Birch Kent was a little slower than he should have been in dropping low again and the bounty hunter on his right homed in on him.

The result was painful.

Birch felt a sudden hot breath of air against his

face and something tugged for the briefest instant at his neck, just above the Adam's apple. At the same instant, there was a loud *thunk* as the bullet embedded itself in a tree trunk barely inches from his face. By the time the thunder of the gun reached his ears, Birch was already diving forward into the channel, tasting river dirt and spitting chunks of debris out of his mouth as he landed.

He was dimly aware of the blood dripping from his throat and mingling with the dirt and leaves. Instinctively, he rolled over on to his back and lay motionless with his Colt in his hand for a few moments. Realizing he could see, feel and cuss without impairment, he decided the wound was not too serious. He had a hunch the ambusher would come to him figuring he was dead. He fingered his bloodied neck: another inch or so and he would have been.

Guns bellowed and men shouted. By the sounds of it, Harlan and Molly were still keeping them busy.

Footsteps were heard!

Gently, Birch thumbed back his gun's hammer.

Twenty feet away, Ted and Jude were closing in, Ted favoring a twisted ankle and Jude bleeding at the shoulder. They were a study in stealth and caution as they halted before the broken stump of an old oak tree.

The bounty hunters had not expected the capture of the escaped convicts to be easy, but neither had they thought it would be so tough. They could not believe Naylor was gone. But they could almost believe Birch Hamilton/Kent was lying dead in the dry channel.

Almost. . . .

'Go ahead,' Jude whispered. 'I got you covered.'

'He is your catch, Jude. You get him and I will cover you,' replied Ted.

'You are quicker than me, Ted,' Jude fired back.

'Not with this bum ankle, I ain't,' cautioned Ted.

Guns roared somewhere behind them. Closer to the river, Naylor lay on his back with arms and legs spread wide, seemingly staring at his henchmen with sightless eyes.

Ted shuddered. 'He is tellin' us to git it finished, Jude – for him.'

Jude motioned with his head. 'Then finish it.' They were not afraid; they were too tough for that. But they were wary old dogs of the bounty hunting trails who did not see any value in taking unnecessary risks. And when it became apparent that neither was prepared to go ahead alone to check on the fugitive, they eased forward together.

They made no sound, but Birch could still 'hear' them. Locked away in the silent confines of the hole in grim Yuma Territorial Prison, he had developed acute hearing that served him well now. He held the Colt against his chest, hands as steady as a rock. And when the untidy top of Ted's head showed above the weedy border of the channel, he made sure he did not miss.

Ted did not even see his quarry lying there. All he saw was the channel, a hellish sunburst of vivid crimson, then total blackness as his limp body sagged against his burly brother-in-arms, almost dragging him down with him.

Birch was on his feet now, his gun spewing fire and lead.

Jude crashed across Ted's body with his bony hands pressed to the agonizing pain in his guts. As he struggled to rise, a shot from another quarter burned across the side of his head, and as he slumped forward, Birch Kent shot him straight through the heart.

The only good bounty hunter – to Birch – was a dead one.

Molly Floyd came running up with a smoking pistol in her hand. 'That was some nice shooting, honey,' Birch complimented her, but she only stared. His shirtfront was soaked in blood. He looked terrible and it was not easy to convince her that his wound looked much worse than it really was.

A sudden upsurge in shooting from deeper in the trees diverted both of their attention. They ran to Harlan's assistance, and found him shot to hell but still fighting off a bounty hunter who was stalking him through the willow trees like a starving wolf. So intent was the killer on his prey that his awareness of danger from behind came with the thunder of Molly's gun and the numb, freezing horror of a bullet-shattered spine.

They left the dying killer for Ethan Harlan, who dragged himself out of cover, holstered his guns and took out his knife.

Molly's eyes widened when she saw the terrible holes in Harlan's torso and back. She looked at Birch, who gently shook his head. Harlan, his close friend of five years of hell, was a dead man. But he had his rights, and Birch would not stand in his way. He watched in silence as Harlan plunged his knife into the bounty hunter's heart before he too, died.

Right then and there, Birch knew the answer to Molly's question. She had asked when he would leave her. The answer was now.

He must go while there was still time – before someone killed him too.

CHAPTER 5

THE CRUELEST LASH

The physical features of Arizona may be described as a series of elevated plateaus, having an altitude of from one hundred feet in the south-west, up to nearly seven thousand feet above sea level, in the north. Mountain ranges, having a general direction of north-west by south-east, extend over this lofty plateau the entire length of the Territory. These mountains often present the appearance of broken and detached spurs, and sometimes occur in regular and continuous ranges. Narrow valleys and wide, open plains lie between the mountains, while deep canyons and gorges, formed by the rains and floods, which sometimes rush with irresistible force from the mountain barriers, cross the country in every direction. The most extensive of these grand mesas, or table lands, is the Colorado Plateau, in the northern portion of the Territory, occupying nearly two-fifths of its entire area.

In the hazy half-light of the dawn, a lone rider was mistily outlined against the pale sky as he halted his mount on top of a soaring ridge above one of those valleys – the Valley of the Sun.

The horseman was broad shouldered and barrel chested with a slender waist any woman might be envious of. He wore a white bandage around his throat and his eyes were deep and clear as they played over the lush Arizona valley.

Birch Hamilton – Kent – had come back to the valley after many years – back to a place to which he had once vowed never to return. He had left behind the outlaw trails, the brawling hell towns, the prisons and the plains and come back, with something to take care of before the bounty hunters tracked him down and killed him like some mangy dog, as they had McBride, Harlan and Lang.

He was sorry they were gone, but hardly stricken. In his world, life was cheap. At least his companions had had one week of freedom before the trouble with the bounty hunters at Cactus Creek. Maybe a week of high living, followed by a courageous end in battle was preferable to life – if it could be called that – in prison. The Valley of the Sun was a long, long way from Yuma Territorial Prison, from Cactus Creek, and even from Molly, who would want him to go north with her to Nevada or Idaho. They knew little about Birch Kent down here; it remained to be seen if they would remember him.

He relaxed in his saddle, hands crossed on the pommel and an unlit cigarette dangling from his lips. There was both expectancy and dread in his expression as his gaze roved over the sprawling vista taking shape in the strengthening light below him.

He had left this place a hurting boy, and come back a wounded man.

They said you could never go home again without finding the place had changed and shrunk, sometimes beyond recognition. He did not find it that way. The valley looked as splendid as it had ever been, the river was as broad and deep, the rolling rangeland just as lush.

To the west, at the richer end of the valley, was a blob of color that was the town of Painted River. Beyond the town lay the wide acres of Alpha Ranch

Birch's mouth felt a little dry as the memories came flooding back. He removed his cigarette, took a swig from his canteen and felt a little better. He lit up, and as he exhaled a cloud of smoke, touched the strapping on his neck and again thought how close it had been. Just a whisker deeper and he would have never returned. . . .

The sun rose as he rode down off the ridge and followed the valley trail. He rode openly, making no attempt at disguise or concealment. He followed the same trail on which he had ridden out that unforgettable day so many years ago . . . and his back itched again.

He would not scratch that itch.

He heeled his mount into a nice trot.

This long-delayed visit might well be his last, he reflected as the horse carried him towards the town. He could not afford to stay long. He thought about heading north to Canada. There were plenty of fat banks and dumb lawmen up there, he thought. It might be fun to play dangerous games with the red-coated Mounties. . . .

But he knew he was only trying to keep his mind off the next hour, the next day . . . It was so long since he had seen them. So much could be changed . . . regrets. . . .

A mile from Painted River, he sighted a rig on the trail ahead. For a moment, Birch held the horse on a tight rein, then eased the pressure. As the gap narrowed, he realized the man and woman riding in the spring cart were complete strangers to him. They nodded and he touched his hat brim as they passed.

The horseman he met a short distance farther along was a man with whom he had gone to school.

'Howdy, stranger,' Birch called.

'Morning, stranger,' the man replied and did not give him a second look.

Birch nodded. Ten years was a long time – an eternity for some.

Painted River had spread out over the years. It was still a nice, solid looking cowtown with no pretensions of being anything else. The false fronts were painted and the citizens looked respectable.

He was home.

At the saloon where he stopped off to buy a drink

and a bottle, the bartender called him *amigo*. Birch did not call the man 'Fred', even though that was his name. It was easy enough for him to identify familiar faces as he sipped his rye whiskey, for he expected them to be familiar. Nobody here would be expecting Birch Kent to show up after the better part of near ten years.

Nearly ten years!

He turned to study himself in the bar mirror. His face was still boyish, but there were harsh lines that dug in deep. He knew it was the kind of face many would find intimidating or scary. There were times when that could be an asset, but he hoped the people he had traveled so far to see would not find him too changed or too 'hard looking'.

'I'm lookin' for work,' he said to the bartender. 'Hear they are hiring out at Alpha Ranch.'

'Guess you heard wrong, mister,' came the cold reply. 'Round up is over and they are layin' off on most spreads.'

'I might go out and see Gentry anyway,' Birch said. 'Big Bruce Gentry. He is still out there, isn't he?'

'Always was and always will be, I reckon. But I still say you will be wastin' your time,' Fred, the bartender said, never stopping wiping the glasses he had before him.

'It is my time to waste,' Birch replied. 'A friend of mine who is a friend of the family was askin' after a woman named Adeline who worked for Gentry.' Birch's manner was casual. 'Is she still in good health?'

The bartender shrugged. 'As far as I know.'

'And ... and there was a girl ... Gentry's niece. . . .'

'That would be Miss Andrea Gentry. A real looker, your friend might have told you that, huh?' Fred's lips hinted at a quick smile.

Birch did not return the smile. 'Matter of fact he did. She OK too?'

Fred shrugged once more. 'Guess so. Want another drink?'

The whiskey was fine but Birch barely tasted it. Adeline and Andrea were both alive and well. That knowledge was more than enough to boost his spirits and help erase the bitterness and trouble at Cactus Creek.

Lifting his glass, he drank a silent toast to McBride, Lang and Harlan, then drank another to whatever gods of fortune had looked after Adeline and Andrea until he had been able to return to the valley.

'You know, mister,' Fred the bartender, said as he refilled Birch's glass, 'Joel here reckons you look kind of familiar.'

Coming out of his reverie, Birch Kent found himself looking at the freckle-spattered face of a bow-legged cowboy with whom he had fought over a girl with pigtails and a lisp.

Birch's face was blank as he said, 'Sorry, you must be gettin' me mixed up with somebody else,' and took his drink to a corner table. He was not interested in reviving old contacts in the valley, only in making it out to the ranch.

Half an hour later, he was on his way again, riding out of Main Street and following the western trail. He was surprised at how calm he felt, all things considered. It seemed to him that he had the rage and hate well bottled up, which of course would be necessary if he was to achieve his purpose here. He allowed the horse to travel at its own pace, and for the next several miles occupied himself identifying familiar landmarks.

Then he reached the Joshua tree where Felder had died.

And that was when the deluge of memories came rushing back in a torrent of emotion that no power could stop. . . .

It was nearly ten years earlier and he was a husky boy of sixteen. His world was cattle, horses and Ranch Town where the Alpha workers lived. He'd been working on the spread since the age of fourteen, already as strong as many of the other men and a good horseman.

It was Big Bruce Gentry's ranch, and he was a larger than life figure in the eyes of Adeline Kent's son. Back then, Birch saw more of Big Bruce than most, as he was a regular visitor to his mother's cabin.

When he was smaller, Birch had often asked about his father, but had long ceased doing so. He had accepted the fact that he was illegitimate – a bastard. He could live with that fact and by the time he was fourteen, other kids stopped teasing him about it.

His fists guaranteed it. A little after his fifteenth birthday, he whipped a full-grown man, a wrangler off Alpha. By the time he was sixteen, he secretly believed he could thrash anyone on the place, with the exception of Big Bruce and his two oversized bodyguards.

Mr Gentry.

Everyone on Alpha called Big Bruce mister. Six feet five and built like a prizefighter, he rode the spread like a king, never popular but always respected – and always with a twelve-foot bullwhip coiled around his shoulder. The whip was for the animals, but Big Bruce was known to use it on men when the spirit moved him to do so. In those days, folk said he could do pretty much as he liked, and nobody dared say otherwise.

Birch had always been curious about Big Bruce's nocturnal visits to his mother's cabin. He would often catch her sitting by her window staring dreamily at the big house on the hill. Later, he would understand why.

The day at the dam was vivid in his memory. He was working with a shovel, helping two others clear silt where drinking cattle were getting bogged down. Stripped to the waist, his broad shoulders glistening with sweat, he glimpsed his mother driving to town in the spring cart and overheard the cowboys' comments.

'There goes the best lookin' female on this or any other spread,' said the first man.

'Better not let Big Bruce catch you talkin' that way

about that woman,' warned the other man. 'That there is his personal property.'

'Do tell?' the first man urged. 'That is the way it is, pal.'

Birch went on digging, but things were falling into place in his mind. A dark place. He was no longer a kid.

His mother was his ideal. A gracious, lovely woman with a fascinating background, she was the only daughter of a rich, southern cotton king, who had seen everything she held dear destroyed during the War between the States. Like so many others of the time, she had finally made her way west to the Valley of the Sun and the sprawling empire of Big Bruce Gentry.

And there she had stayed, working as a servant at the house, living in Ranch Town and rearing a son – her fatherless son.

The boy grew up with horses and cattle and as he developed towards manhood, became more skilled with both every day.

There were fights and Birch Kent always won – each and every one of them. He was not aggressive by nature, but would not let anyone push him around or put anything over on him. And that included Hugh Legler and Frank Wise.

Big Bruce's bodyguards were young men at the time, husky giants hired by the cattle king following an attempt on his life by a disgruntled ex-employee. Wherever Big Bruce went, Legler and Wise accompanied him, whether on the spread, in the town, or during his many trips away on business.

Legler, the bigger of the two men and commonly regarded as the tougher of the two, was a black-haired man with arms as thick as most men's legs and with a surprising grace and speed to his movements.

It was Hugh Legler who got tough with Birch on that long-ago summer's day when Andrea Gentry visited his mother in Ranch Town.

Andrea Gentry's parents had died in a fire back in Chicago and the family had packed her off west to live with her uncle. She was delicate and flower-like with long, golden hair and a developing figure that promised to be sensational. She liked Adeline, and Birch sensed she also liked him. He certainly admired her. She was so different from the girls of Ranch Town or Painted River that she might have been from a foreign land or another world for all he knew.

They strolled around the town that lazy Sunday afternoon as birds chirped and sunlight poured like molten gold across the Alpha acres – young, innocent and just enjoying themselves.

There was no harm in it, no possible harm. Yet suddenly, big Legler was there, dark-faced and angry, accusing Birch of 'getting ideas above himself' – whatever in hell that meant.

'I'm takin' Miss Andrea back to the house, kid,' he growled and gave Birch a shove. 'And don't let me see you with her again. Understand?'

That was just the point. Birch did not understand. What was the bodyguard getting so excited about?

'What is wrong about me showing Andrea around?' Birch had asked. 'Where is the harm in that?'

'Don't gimme any backchat, kid,' Legler snapped. 'Now, get the hell back to your mommy's shack and mind your manners. Come along, Miss Gentry.'

'Wait.'

Birch's face went pale. The sight of Legler's big, hairy hand on Andrea's shoulder had a strange effect on him. He had been angry before, but this was completely different. This kind of cold rage seemed to spring from somewhere deep within him. All his life, people had sought to convey the impression that he was low class and less important than other boys and girls who had both mothers and fathers. Until that day, he had always been able to live with that. But now someone else was involved, and he would not be shamed before Andrea Gentry.

'Just hang on a lousy minute, Legler,' he had said in a strained voice. 'I still want to know where the harm is.'

'Oh, you do, do you?' Legler inflated his chest and pointed an accusing finger. 'Well, it is simple enough, boy. This here is Mr Gentry's niece and he does not want her runnin' with the likes of you – a bastard. Is that plain enough for you, kid?'

Birch clenched his fists. He had been called that ugly name before and thought he was conditioned to it. But it took on a new dimension when he heard it in the company of the girl.

Andrea, for her part, was offended. 'You really are

67

very ill-mannered, Mr Legler,' she chided in her edu-
cated Eastern voice. 'I shall have to speak to Uncle
Bruce about you.'

Hugh Legler gnawed his lower lip. He dared not
say anything to the girl – despite wanting to – but
Birch was different.

'If you get me into trouble with Big Bruce, kid, you
will regret it, I guarantee you that.' Again, he put his
hand on Andrea's shoulder. 'Miss Gentry?'

'Take your dirty hand off her.' Birch was very
angry, unreasonably so. It was more than Legler's
interference in his pleasure. He felt he was being
made to look like a second-rate nothing in front of
someone who was important to him. He approached
the hulking bodyguard and faced him squarely. 'I
might be a bastard,' he heard himself say, 'but I am
not a piece of scum like you!'

Legler let fly with an uppercut that might well
have lifted Birch's head off, had it connected. But he
avoided the punch and slammed a hard fist straight
into the big man's mouth, drawing blood. Birch
heard Andrea gasp as Legler staggered. Then the
man righted himself and rushed ferociously at
Birch.

They stood toe to toe slugging it out as people
came running from all over to watch. There was no
way Birch could get on top of a professional bruiser
who outweighed him by some fifty or more pounds,
but by the same token, Hugh Legler found himself
incapable of getting the best of Birch. What he
lacked in size, weight and reach he made up for in

speed, striking power and sheer ferocity. Both combatants were bleeding, cut and breathing hard by the time Gentry arrived from the house.

Birch sighted the big man from the corner of his eye. He kept fighting, but Legler suddenly dropped his arms and stepped back, looking towards his employer. Birch's eyes darted to Andrea. She was watching him with what appeared to be fearful admiration. Birch took two lightning steps forward and crashed an overhand right to Legler's unprotected jaw. The bodyguard fell like a sack of wheat.

It was not an honorable victory, but it was a victory nonetheless. The crowd appeared stunned. Big Bruce Gentry looked good and mad.

'And just what the hell do you think you two are doing?'

The question was directed straight at the youthful Birch. Gentry rarely addressed him, and Birch had always had the impression that his mother's friend did not like him very much. He did everything he could do to impress Big Bruce, but it never seemed to work. Birch had come to accept it, although he did not understand it. Gentry had never spoken to him like this before, and while he was trying to frame a reply, the rancher told him plainly where he stood.

'This is Alpha Ranch, not some low dive, boy! You do your brawling elsewhere in the future, otherwise you will find yourself off this ranch. Do you understand me?'

Birch nodded. They collected the dazed Legler and headed for the house. Some men came up to slap him on the back and praise him for his win. He ignored them. He was watching the way Andrea's hair caught the sunlight as she made for the house on the hill.

Several weeks later, Big Bruce came to the cabin. Birch had been out in the hills, hunting a wolf with friends. When he walked in, he saw Adeline dabbing her eyes. His gaze went accusingly to Gentry who rose and left without another word.

Later that night, Adeline Kent told her son that Big Bruce Gentry was his father, but the rancher would never acknowledge that fact.

The weeks went slowly that summer, which was destined to be Birch's last on Alpha. Big Bruce's wife, Laura, was a regular visitor to the cabin; she and Adeline were close friends, and if the woman knew about Birch's parentage, she never gave a sign.

Sometimes Andrea accompanied Mrs Gentry to the cabin, and they were the best times of all. The children – and that was all they were – grew close. Birch learned that Andrea loved her aunt, but not her uncle. Andrea almost seemed to fear Big Bruce, but Birch had no idea why until, one day, he overheard the ranch hands discussing the Gentrys in a way that suggested Big Bruce lusted after his teenage niece.

This seemed too outlandish for Birch to accept, but later, when he hinted at what he had heard to his mother, she became angry with him for one of the rare times in his life. He never mentioned the whispers and gossip again, either to her or to Andrea.

The summer was coming to a close and there was a chill in the morning air. Adeline Kent, never strong, contracted pneumonia in the first weeks of fall and Laura Gentry ordered her brought to the house where she could be properly looked after.

Although deeply concerned about his mother, this suited Birch admirably, for it enabled him to visit the house frequently and see much more of Andrea.

If Big Bruce was aware of their deepening friendship, he gave no sign. He continued to treat Birch with frigid remoteness. Legler took Birch aside once to warn him against getting any fancy notions about Miss Andrea. Birch ignored him. Legler hated him now, and the feeling was mutual.

One afternoon in the fall, while showing off for Andrea, Birch carried a three-hundred-pound sack of corn across the ranch yard on his shoulders. Later, both Legler and Wise secretly attempted to emulate the feat and failed.

This bastard boy of Adeline Kent's was hardly a boy any longer.

CHAPTER 6

THE BASTARD BOY

The day Birch would never forget dawned clear and cold. It was a Sunday, the traditional day of rest on Alpha Ranch, and as usual, he hitched Old Nathan to the buggy and drove his mother to church in Painted River. Andrea was there, looking beautiful, and Laura Gentry. Big Bruce never attended church.

Afterwards, the little group took lunch at the diner, and Birch was once again made aware of how much Mrs Gentry liked both him and Adeline.

'Just look at how this boy of yours is growing, Adeline,' she said over the cakes and coffee. 'So handsome and strong.'

Birch blushed and Andrea was amused. But Adeline was only proud as she rested her hand on his arm.

'He is my strength, Laura,' she said. 'I know

nothing really bad will ever happen to me as long as I have my boy.'

And Birch felt good, while at the same time puzzled that, under the circumstances, the two women could be friends. Laura Gentry was in poor health, yet very intelligent and perceptive. It was not possible, Birch thought, that she did not know about Adeline and her husband and could not be aware that he was Big Bruce's son.

It seemed strange to him that Laura did not resent the Kents. She had every reason to do so, yet it was plain she regarded them as friends.

Birch spent the long, sunny afternoon that followed their return to Alpha tossing horseshoes with his friends and breaking in the new horse he had saved up for, and bought from the wrangler.

He was riding the horse down the river trail when he sighted Sheriff Rigdon Elliott coming in from the hills on his handsome black, leading an appaloosa.

Birch grinned. Painted River's tall, sober lawman was probably the man he admired most. He was strong, solid and different from Big Bruce Gentry in every way that mattered.

Birch was not surprised to discover that Elliott had recovered John Dennen's stolen appaloosa, for it was said around the valley that whenever the sheriff went after somebody or something, he never came back empty handed.

The lawman and the boy talked for some time in the cool, willow shade before Birch invited him back to Ranch Town for coffee.

Elliott accepted readily. Like most of the men Birch knew, the sheriff was an admirer of his mother, but certainly no admirer of Big Bruce.

Andrea arrived late in the afternoon after Elliott had left. And that was where it began . . . Strolling out to look at the sunset, the kisses, the hayloft in the barn, Big Bruce walking in on them, the whip. . . .

Birch was cut to pieces and half dead when he finally escaped Ranch Town. But not content with what he had done, Gentry sent his bodyguards out to find him. He wanted Birch brought back and turned over to the law to face charges. That night, Big Bruce Gentry was like a man possessed.

The Joshua tree. . . .

The bleeding, hunted boy made it that far before Legler, Wise, and James Felder, Gentry's hardcase trio, ran him down. But it was dark, the bodyguards were over-eager, and Birch was desperate and dangerous. In the gloom, he got around behind Legler, knocked him unconscious with a rock and took his gun.

Felder came running, pistol in his hand, fire in his eyes, and murder in his heart.

Birch shot him through the heart, took his horse and had been on the dodge ever since.

Now he was back before the Joshua tree, feeling every deep scar on his back, recalling every moment of pain and bewilderment.

At last he shook his head and rode on to the sign-post that read:

RANCH TOWN 2 MILES
ALPHA RANCH HOUSE 3 MILES

He reached Ranch Town, and found the cabin boarded up and deserted. Old Mother Cheever, the first person to recognize the husky man as the fresh-faced boy who had left ten years earlier, told him the news. Adeline now lived at the house on the hill. She was Mrs Gentry now: she had married Big Bruce Gentry after Laura had died. Didn't Birch know?

He sure as hell didn't.

'Why, Ma?'

His mother replied simply, 'He asked me, Birch.'

'And that was all it took to get you to marry him?' Birch was still confused.

'More than that, my darling boy . . . much more than that. But we will discuss that later. Just let me look at you. I can't believe how you have changed! You look strong enough to take on the whole world, Birch.'

She hugged him and he felt his anger melting away. It was not hard to understand. After all, he had left her with nothing but an empty cabin. Sure, he had sent money when he could, but Adeline would have been desperately lonely without him. And after all, she and Big Bruce had been lovers.

Adeline had aged well. Always beautiful, she was now gray and thinner than before, but regal-looking and calm. Seated at the rough kitchen table in Mother Cheever's shack in Ranch Town, where she had come to meet him, to her son, she looked like a queen with tears of happiness in her eyes.

I don't really care, he told himself. I don't really care that she shares her bed with the son of a bitch who sired me, but would not acknowledge me, who damn near murdered me and ruined my life. It is what was good for Ma that mattered. . . .

He learned that Big Bruce was away on business, accompanied by Legler and Wise. The bodyguards still rode for the rancher after all this time.

When Birch asked her if she was happy, his mother replied evasively that she was now. Where had he been all these years?

The lies came easily and plausibly. Nobody down here connected Birch Kent with the wild outlaw, Birch Hamilton. Here in the Valley of the Sun, he was a clean skin. Yuma Territorial Prison was many hundreds of miles from Mother Cheever's shack in Ranch Town. They may have heard about the trouble at Cactus Creek between the Hamilton gang and the bounty hunters, but it would mean nothing at all to them.

Adeline took his hands. 'You won't leave again, will you, Birch?'

'You know I can't stay here, Ma,' he said directly.

'Bruce has forgotten all about you.'

He gritted his teeth then said, 'But I haven't forgotten about him.'

She squeezed his hands tightly. 'Darling, I can talk to him. He listens to me. I can patch things up between you. You were always so good with horses and cattle. You could get yourself a quarter section in

76

the valley and. . . .'

'No, Ma . . . I couldn't. . . .'

Two things prevented him from considering her proposal. One was a past that would surely catch up with him sooner or later. The other was his hate. Adeline was married to Big Bruce, but that did not stop Birch hating him. There had been long, frozen nights in solitary confinement when he had kept himself going only by remembering how much he hated his father. He would hate him until his dying breath. That was how things were, and nothing could change it.

'I beg of you, Birch. If only you knew how I have missed you. . . .'

'You have got your husband, Ma.'

Adeline released his hands and turned away from him. 'I hate him,' she said. 'If possible, I hate him more than you do, my boy.'

Birch was astonished.

'Hate him? But you married him?'

'I had my reasons.'

'But you and him go way back, Ma. Twenty-five years or more.'

Adeline's eyes were tragic now, her serenity gone.

'I was a woman alone when I came west, Birch, totally alone. I had no skills. Like so many others, I came west following a dream that became a nightmare.' She shrugged. 'In the end, I had two choices – either to sell myself, or take up with Bruce. I took the easier way.'

Birch nodded slowly and was about to answer

when he heard the horse. Looking through the window, he saw a lovely woman in riding gear reining in by the cabin. She sprang to the ground and leapt up on to the porch, her face alive with excitement as she called his name: 'Birch? Birch, it is me!'

The next moment, Andrea was in his massive arms.

'What the hell is going on here?' demanded Big Bruce Gentry, striding into the lamplit room where the housekeeper was setting supper for one. 'Where is my wife and Miss Andrea?'

The plump, motherly woman shook her head. 'I don't know, Mr Gentry. They left the house this afternoon and have not been back.'

'Legler!' Gentry bellowed, striding to the liquor cabinet and selecting a bottle. 'Legler, get in here, dammit man!'

The man who appeared in the doorway was the only person in the valley taller than Big Bruce himself. Hugh Legler was almost fifteen years younger than his boss. He was an arrogant, cruel man who, nonetheless, sometimes allowed himself to be treated like a lackey. There was a reason for this. Legler liked his life on Alpha Ranch and always had. Any place else, he would have had to work for a living. Here, all he had to do was watch out for Gentry's safety and follow orders unquestioningly.

'They are not here,' Big Bruce complained loudly, gulping down straight rye. 'Where in tarnation would they be?'

'Want me to look for them, boss?' Legler asked.

'Pour me another,' his large employer ordered.

It pleased Gentry to have big, strong men run after him; it made him feel good. He had always been the most powerful man in the Valley of the Sun, and that, too, pleased him. But that did not mean Big Bruce Gentry was a happy man. He was not. No man who wanted as much as he did could ever be really satisfied. And no matter how much he acquired, it was never enough.

Grabbing his drink, he led the way through to his study. The shelves were lined with unread books, unappreciated works of art decorated the walls. Bruce Gentry surrounded himself with all the trappings of wealth and success because it was expected of him. But he would rather roll in the hay with a hot-blooded harlot than read Poe or Dickens any day of the week.

'Women!' he said with a look of bitterness in his mouth. 'Indulge them and pamper them and they have no idea what is expected of them in return. They know I hate coming home to an empty house.'

There were six servants and two bodyguards resident at the house, but Legler knew what he meant.

'It is not like Mrs Gentry to be away from the place, boss,' he said guardedly.

From his desk, Big Bruce glanced up at him with bloodshot eyes. That look said it all. It wasn't his wife Big Bruce was concerned about, and both men were well aware of that fact.

It had always amused Legler to stand back and

observe his master's unrequited infatuation with his lovely niece, or that a woman in Andrea's position could prove so resolutely stubborn. Big Bruce had often threatened to throw her off Alpha, but had never gone through with it. Legler suspected it might even be true love, at least on Big Bruce's part, but Andrea obviously felt nothing but dislike for her uncle.

'That uppity bitch!' Big Bruce was in a foul mood tonight. His business dealing had not gone well. He was tired, irritable and drinking far too much. He rarely spoke out against Andrea, not even to Legler and Wise, but his anger loosened his tongue. 'How long has she been here, Legler?'

'Almost ten years, boss,' Legler obediently answered.

'Ten years! My lord! Have I been waiting for her that long?'

Legler might have reminded his employer that he had had two wives in that time, which might have accounted for his lack of success with Andrea, but decided against that notion. He could tell Gentry wanted to talk, and, as always, allowed him the floor.

'Long time, boss,' was all Legler managed to say.

'You don't know what it is like,' Gentry said darkly. 'To be tied to old women and want a young one. And a young one like her . . . Judas!'

Legler knew what he meant. There was something about Andrea that would attract any man. She was at once lovely, spirited and unattainable. Legler sensed it might be the latter quality that most fascinated Gentry.

'Well, you have always got Susana, boss. She is young,' Legler offered.

Big Bruce dismissed his Painted River whore with a gesture. 'I am discussing women, not whores.' He drained his glass and signaled for another. Lamplight gleamed on the bottle as Legler poured another shot of whiskey. Big Bruce's mood grew deeper and darker. 'Women! The beauty and the bane of life, Legler. Who would have believed Laura would have crossed me the way she did? Imagine that rich bitch leaving half Alpha Ranch to my mistress! Can you believe the bitterness that must have inspired her to do a thing like that?'

Legler smiled inwardly. The reason Big Bruce was rich was simple. He had married money. He had spent his entire married life with Laura trying to separate her from her lands and cash, but had only partially succeeded. Upon her death, Laura had left half her wealth to Gentry and the other half to Adeline Kent. Naturally, Big Bruce had been obliged to marry Adeline in order to keep 'his' empire together. He was now endeavoring to persuade her to sign over her half to him, but she was proving as obdurate as Laura had been.

It always amused Legler when he saw his boss confronted with obstacles he could not overcome. It made up for a lot of the abuse he had to take from him.

Big Bruce continued to ramble on in the same vein before the chiming of a clock reminded him of the passage of time.

'Still not back,' he barked, getting up. 'Go find

81

them, Legler. Now.'

'Sure thing, boss.' Legler went to the door. 'What about Wise?'

'He had better stay here with me . . . in case.' Big Bruce was a man who really needed protection due to all the enemies he had created. He collected enemies like a philatelist collected stamps. 'Don't come back without them . . . understand?'

Hugh Legler met Wise at the front door. The two heavyweights had worked together for so long they were like brothers – blood brothers.

'Looks like we are in for a long night,' Legler said, putting on his hat. 'He is on the rye and mean.'

'So, nothing new about that.' Six-foot two Wise had a scarred, curiously blank face. Good with both gun and knife, he was reliable when the chips were down.

'Yeah, what is new?' Legler scowled. 'Any idea where Adeline and Andrea could be?'

'I was talkin' to the yard man. He says Old Mother Cheever was up here earlier this afternoon. Seems Mrs Gentry left shortly after. She could be down in Ranch Town.'

'I will go check it out.' Legler jerked his head. 'You had better get in there. I think he wants someone to tell his troubles to.'

Wise's scarred face creased in a half-smile as he went inside. The bodyguards were pleased when their employer was having a bad time. Yet they never dared let it show, for, rugged characters though they were, each man maintained a healthy fear of Big

Bruce, who played rough when it suited him – rougher than they knew how.

Wise heard his partner's horse gallop away as he reached the study.

CHAPTER 7

THE BASTARD IS BACK!

The wanted poster read:

WANTED!
FOR MURDER, ROBBERY, AND JAILBREAK
BIRCH HAMILTON SIX FOOT,
AUBURN HAIR, BROWN EYES.
A STRONG BUILD. WHEREABOUTS
UNKNOWN.
$2,000 REWARD
DEAD OR ALIVE

The drawing accompanying the notice was crudely executed, yet the likeness was unmistakable, even if Birch did not like how it looked. The face staring back from the yellowed paper at Adeline and Andrea was identical to the one looking at them across the table.

'I had to tell you,' Birch said.

This was the moment he had dreaded. Yet when he looked at them, he knew he need not have worried. There was no censure in their faces, no condemnation. All he could see was understanding.

It was Adeline who spoke first.

'I guessed you would become a fugitive after what happened to James Felder, Birch,' she said gently.

Birch shrugged and looked down. 'I was a killer.'

'Rigdon Elliott saw it differently, Birch,' Andrea said. 'But, of course, it was too late by then.'

Painted River's former sheriff had gone far since the old days, more of a friend to Birch than an enemy. Elliott had continued to pay occasional visits to his mother.

Elliott had never revealed to Adeline any details of Birch's exploits or his alias, and for that Birch would always be grateful. But he realized now that he and the marshal had rarely discussed the violent events here in the valley that had driven him from his home and on to the owl hoot trail.

'How did the marshal see it, Andrea?' he asked.

Adeline answered the question.

'Rigdon said that the men Big Bruce sent after you that night did not constitute a posse. They were not deputized and had no authority to pursue you. Therefore, when they tried to kill you, you had the legal right to defend yourself.'

Birch understood now why Elliott had never told

him this. It would have been hard to take, for it had been the assumption that he was a killer in the eyes of the law that had driven him to adopt an alias and live as an outlaw. How different his life might have been had he known the truth back then!

It was far too late now.

Yet now he had made a clean breast of his past, he felt good because they were not condemning him.

It was growing late. He knew there were some risks involved in his overstaying his welcome, yet could not drag himself away. And when Adeline suggested that he and Andrea might like a little time alone, he jumped at the chance.

They strolled together down to the creek, observed only by the stars in the sky.

'It is lovely to see you again, Birch.'

'You too. . . .' Birch was thinking about Molly. They were the same, he and Molly. Andrea was different. She had been a gentle lady when they had met, and had remained that way. She had not condemned the way of life he had chosen, but he knew it had opened up a vast chasm between them. Not that it mattered greatly, he told himself. What had existed between himself and the lovely young woman at his side was long gone. Too much blood had been spilt since then. Andrea would one day marry some upstanding, well-to-do young man whose only knowledge of outlawry would come from what he read in the papers or dime novels. Indeed, he was surprised she had not yet found a suitable man. Or perhaps she had?

He asked her as they sat on a log in the moonlight, and Andrea's face darkened with sadness.

'I am afraid I am going to be a dried up old spinster, Birch,' she said.

He shook his head. 'I find that hard to believe.'

'It is the truth,' she replied.

'You mean there is no one in your life? No man?' He was surprised.

'Yes, that is what I am saying.'

'What is wrong with the men around these parts? Don't they know class when they see it?' He was flabbergasted.

Andrea smiled, but still her face showed sadness. 'You always said I had class. Do you still believe that to be true, Birch?'

'No.'

His answered shocked the woman. 'Oh. . . ?'

'I don't think it, I know it.'

'You are so sweet. But then, you always were to me,' she said.

'If I was, it was easy enough. But come on, Andrea, tell me why they haven't been knocking the doors down to get to you . . .' he supplied.

She wasn't smiling now as she studied the slow-moving waters. 'There have been a couple of serious suitors, Birch. But they are not around anymore.'

He looked puzzled. 'Why not?'

'Perhaps I should not bother telling you . . .' she began.

Birch frowned. 'Why not? What harm will it do? I am a big boy; I can take it.'

87

'Do you still hate him for what he did to you?'

He was gazing at the lights on the hill. 'For want of a better word, hate will do. But what has he got to do with what you are tellin' me?'

Andrea was silent for a long moment. Then she said, 'I suppose you have a right to know. The truth is, Birch, Uncle Bruce doesn't allow me to have any serious suitors.'

Birch stared. 'Doesn't allow?' He began to boil inside. 'How is that? Why not?'

She turned her face away from him. 'You have no idea.'

He wasn't sure if she meant that as a shot at his intelligence or something else. 'I might be dumb, but no, I haven't any idea why.'

She had not meant to upset him or to make him feel stupid. 'He . . . he wants me for' – she paused, almost afraid to finish the sentence – 'himself.'

Something plopped into the creek, and an ancient, gray owl stared down with yellow eyes at the couple. Birch had a strange sensation of time slowing down to enable him to catch up. Gentry wanted Andrea . . . it sounded unreal at first, but less so as he thought about it.

Big Bruce had always been a womanizer; he was notorious for it around the valley. The word was that no good-looking female was truly safe from Big Bruce Gentry. Adeline and Laura had been handsome women, while Andrea was a beautiful woman. But she was thirty or more years his junior.

He shook his head. 'How do you feel about him?'

The words tasted awful as he spoke them.

'I despise him. And if you are wondering why I don't leave, I have no place to go, Birch. Bruce knows that, and makes sure he keeps me poor and dependent on him. He thinks I will weaken and submit to him one day, but of course, I never shall.'

Birch rubbed his jaw. Inside him, the hate burned white-hot. The scars on his back ached. It was as though the clock had been turned back ten years and he was an angry boy in a blood-soaked shirt staggering through the brush, sobbing with uncontrolled rage.

'And this is the man my mother married,' he breathed. 'I still can't come to terms with that, you know, Andrea. I know she was poor and lonely . . . but to marry him!'

'Perhaps Adeline had reasons you don't know or understand.'

He turned to her sharply, startling her. 'Like what, Andrea?'

She looked away. 'It is not my place to tell you. . . .'

They stopped talking at the sound of hoofbeats. A towering figure was riding into Ranch Town from the hill trail. Ten years had not affected Birch's memory. He recognized Legler – one of the men who had stripped him and lashed him to the barn door for the flogging.

'We have stayed too long, Birch,' Andrea said. 'If the guards are back, that means Big Bruce is back too. He has sent Legler looking for us. I will have to go, Birch.'

Birch Kent did not reply. He was watching Hugh Legler dismount and walk across to inspect his horse.

Adeline emerged from the house. Birch heard Legler's voice and knew he was asking her about the horse.

At that moment, Birch made a decision. He was not going to hide and skulk about. He had a right to see his mother after all this time. He started up the slope swiftly, with Andrea running after him.

'No, Birch!' she cried. 'They must not know you are here!'

'Too late,' he replied grimly. 'He has already seen me.'

Then he called out. 'Keep your lousy paw away from that gun, or you might have to use it, Legler.' He felt almost exhilarated. He had left a boy and come back a man. He would never be as big as his father or his bodyguards, but he was ready to bet money he was harder.

Legler's hand slid away from his gun butt as Birch came striding into the light issuing from Mother Cheever's window. He was hatless and stood broad-shouldered and erect, looking like a tougher proposition than a man of mere flesh and bone.

'Judas Priest!' Hugh Legler breathed. 'The bastard is back!'

The confrontation that had been ten years coming, took place some ten minutes later right there in the bright moonlight outside Mother Cheever's shack, when Gentry and Wise rode down to Ranch Town to check on what was delaying Legler.

They found him by the front porch with Adeline, Andrea and Big Bruce's rugged son.

'You!' Big Bruce could not believe his eyes. 'I thought you were dead, boy.'

'You will die long before me,' Birch predicted, but Adeline stepped in.

'Birch, Bruce,' she cried. 'Don't let us have any trouble. The past is the past and we can't. . . .'

'Take him!' Big Bruce snarled, making a violent gesture to his men. 'We are taking him in to hang for the murder of the fella Felder!'

Birch had not expected Gentry to have changed, but he was not quite prepared for this unbridled hostility, and thought, almost admiringly, *Why, the son of a bitch hates me almost as much as I hate him!*

'You heard the man,' scar-faced Wise growled, dismounting. 'Hand over that hogleg. '

'For God's sake, Bruce,' Adeline cried, 'you can't do this. Birch only came back to visit with me.'

'Don't fool yourself, woman,' Gentry's voice was like a file. He jabbed a finger at Andrea. 'That is *who* brought him back from under whatever rock he has been hiding these ten years, not you, Adeline.'

It was true, Birch thought, what Andrea had said. Bruce Gentry's jealousy was blatantly apparent. It was jealousy that had seen him take the whip to him that day, jealousy that was fueling him now. He was like a man possessed. Birch had seen enough of that kind in his time to recognize all the signs.

'Well, what are you waiting for?' Gentry yelled. 'Do

as you are told! Carry out your orders.'

Birch noted that Wise seemed eager, while big Legler held back. He had always rated Legler as the more intelligent of the pair, and this proved it. It seemed Hugh Legler was quicker to recognize the changes in Birch than his partner was. He certainly was not afraid, but he was cautious.

Wise, the professional stand-over artist and gun-fighter was not troubled by any such uncertainties. 'You should have stayed away, mister,' he said, advancing, his knife-scarred face pale in the moon-light. 'You are gonna be mighty sorry you didn't, I am thinkin'.'

Birch did not move. He had lost count of the number of times he had faced a man with the scent of death in the air. In Yuma Territorial Prison, you learned to win at any cost or go under, and he had never gone under.

'You had better back up, Wise.' Birch warned.

Wise momentarily reacted to the quiet threat in those words and came to a halt. But as Gentry started to curse, Wise shrugged and came on, holding out his hand for the six-shooter he was not going to get.

Not in his hand, leastwise.

Birch waited until the big man was almost upon him before he drew. The gun came out with such speed that Wise had no opportunity to go for his own weapon. And the barrel struck so hard and fast, he had no chance to duck. There was a sodden thud and big Wise measured his length in the dust with blood oozing from a deep gash in his forehead.

'I warned him,' Birch announced, holstering his gun. 'A man can't do more than that.'

Big Bruce Gentry was red-faced with rage. He ruled here and had done so for a very long time that nobody dared challenge his authority – or had not until now.

He grabbed the handle of the whip coiled around his saddle horn and as he dismounted, it straightened with an evil, sibilant hiss.

For Birch, that sound was like a key that unlocked a Pandora's box of memories. He was transported back in time ten years to when he had been a kid with a kid's fears and uncertainties. A boy in a man's world, he was confronted by the giant figure of his father and his outsized protectors. They overpowered him and stripped off his shirt. Andrea was sobbing as he heard the whispering hiss of that whip snaking through the air. There was one hanging moment of anticipation, then the searing pain of contact.

It was all so vivid and fresh.

But he was not a boy any longer. He was a man.

This was man against man. Father against son. Hate versus hate. Strength versus strength.

The way Birch moved left the onlookers breathless. Empty-handed and ignoring the towering Legler, he charged at Gentry as the lash leapt out. His right hand moving with the speed of a striking rattler, Birch snatched hold of the flying lash. He jerked at it with all his strength, hauling Gentry towards him.

The rancher tried to dig in with his heels, but Birch was inexorable. His strength of purpose was such that he might well have hauled a locomotive off the tracks at that moment. He heard his mother cry out, and was dimly aware of Andrea watching, frozen, from the porch. Dust boiled from Big Bruce's boots as his heels left twin furrows behind him. The big man's face was mottled with rage as he found himself being dragged right up to his son where they stood chest to chest for an unforgettable second.

'It is your turn, old man,' Birch snarled and slammed his knee into Big Bruce's groin and the big man grunted in pain.

It was a terrible blow. Big Bruce's face turned a deathly shade of gray and he moaned sickly as his legs refused to support him and he began to fall.

Birch's pistol jumped into his fist and spewed fire and smoke as Legler, standing almost directly behind Gentry, went for his gun. The bullet slammed into the giant's shoulder, knocking him off his feet almost under the horses' hoofs and making them rear in fright.

Birch shoved the smoking muzzle of his pistol into Gentry's ashen face as the rancher came to rest on his knees. 'Beg, you son of a bitch!' He was enjoying himself. This was the dream that had sustained him and now it was reality. He had come back to Alpha Ranch as a man, seeking vengeance for the suffering he had endured as a boy and he finally succeeded.

Frank Wise was groaning in the dust as he began to regain his senses. Hugh Legler was slumped on the bottom step of the cabin clutching a bloodied shoulder, and best of all, Big Bruce was crouched on his knees in the dust before him, unable to rise. But he would not beg, and staring into his eyes, Birch could see the hatred still burning there intensely.

'You were born scum and you will die the same,' Birch said, holstering his pistol. 'You treat human beings like cattle and you think you are some kind of god. I am here to tell you – no, show you – what a miserable, gutless son of a bitch you truly are at heart. Throw me out? Reject me? What made you think I would ever want to claim you as my own blood? All I have in life is a mother, you scum. All I ever wanted was that. She married you, and that is her cross to bear. If she married the devil, she would still be my mother. But you? You are a filthy pig and you are going to shout it to the world – now.'

Birch Kent picked up the whip. It gave him some pleasure but not as much as the look on his father's face.

Big Bruce Gentry's face went even paler.

Birch's mother cried out, but nothing could stop the terrible blow. The sleek lash hissed through the dusty air and Gentry's hickory shirt was sliced in half as the stroke landed across his chest, shoulder and back in a bloody strike.

Indeed, the blow was so extremely hard that, as blood spurted and Birch drew back the whip for another stroke, Gentry's eyes rolled in their sockets and he fell face forward on the ground, unconscious.

Then Adeline was standing before her son. He was

angry with her for interfering, but, of course, any anger he might feel against his mother was a pin-prick compared to the emotion that had held him in its grip for the past few minutes.

Slowly he allowed the whip to slide from his hand. Reason returned and the murderous look disappeared from his eyes. He placed an arm around Adeline's shoulders and walked her across to Andrea, feeling drained and almost spent as the emotion left him.

He had not planned the confrontation but realized that, deep down, he had known it could happen and had prepared himself to meet it head on.

Ranch hands were riding down from the house on the hill, drawn by the shot.

Once again, it was time for him to say goodbye. He had overstayed his welcome as he often did.

CHAPTER 8

HAVEN FOR
RUFFIANS

The grubby man who rode into Huachua Hills, near the border of Arizona and Nevada, that afternoon was surprised and stimulated to see a handsome female seated all alone on the hotel porch, who smoked a cigar and looked very bored.

A trapper from the hills who came down once a month to kick up his heels, the hairy man was accustomed to shop-soiled percentage girls and two-dollar whores who were about all Huachua Hills had to offer. But this was something different; this was class.

'Ferget it, Harvey,' counseled the bum who took charge of his horse at the saloon. 'She's pizen.'

'What do you mean?' drooled Harvey the trapper, spitting on his palms to slick back his greasy hair in what he mistakenly believed to be a stylish fashion.

'Pizen? That there is the sweetest lookin' dish I ever did see and—'

'She is all alone, Harvey,' the man broke in. 'Ain't you noticed that?'

'So?' Harvey the trapper was busily knocking clouds of dust off his verminous clothing with his battered hat.

'So, there is a reason fer that.'

'You mean she is choosy?' His horse did not reply to the question.

He shook his head. 'Nope.'

'What, then?'

He paused, looked at the horse. 'Homicidal.'

Harvey the trapper looked a little peeved. 'Are you cracked or somethin'? Do you know what homicidal means?'

'Sure, it means murderous. And that is precisely what that one is, partner. Don't mess with her, I am a warnin' you.'

But Harvey the trapper could not accept that. He was a red-blooded, all-American male, desperately starved of feminine affection, who was ready to drink muddy water and sleep in a hollow log if he did not get some company real soon. And as he made his eager, bowlegged way to the hotel, he realized that the closer he got, the more desirable she became. Goddammit, this here female made Lanie Smith look downright homely!

Molly, who had occupied the same chair on the porch for several days, ever since putting a bullet through the Stetson of the last Romeo to offer to change her life into a golden fantasy of unendurable pleasure, saw the newcomer from the corner of her eye and sighed. The male ego, she thought. It was as vast as the Great Plains and at least as high as the Rockies. What made them all think they were God's gift to women? She suspected this one didn't even have any teeth in his mouth.

She was right about that. Harvey the trapper had no more teeth than a Rhode Island Red. But he refused to believe that choppers were a necessity when it came to romance. Sweeping off his sorry hat, he smiled a broad, toothless smile.

'Ma'am, I have the honor and distinction of bein' Harvey Lyles,' whose usual approach in matters of romance consisted of a blunt, 'How about it, honey?' But it left this raven-haired beauty cold.

She said softly, 'Get your ragged ass off my porch before I set it alight.'

Harvey blinked, certain his hearing was playing tricks on him. Women just did not talk that way, he told himself. Certainly, not to him.

'I don't believe you heard me right, ma'am, I said. . . .'

'I heard you just fine. I heard you loud and clear,' Molly drawled. 'And you sound like a bull bear pukin' in a rain barrel. Now, vamoose!'

Harvey the trapper straightened. A man had his pride, and his was offended. 'Are you drunk, ma'am?'

Molly leaned toward him. 'Get lost, you bum,' she said clearly and distinctly.

99

'By God and by Judas, I don't have to take this . . .' Harvey started to say.

'Yes, you do, you toothless son of a bitch. You will take this and more. And do you know why? Because you are the most unappetizing, seedy, ugly and unfortunate excuse for a man these eyes have ever seen. And worst of all, you are blocking my view. Get lost before I get peeved.'

With a roar of outrage, Harvey the trapper reached for Molly, and Molly went for her gun.

The blast that shook the street sent Harvey reeling backwards clutching his leathery cheek where he now sported a black powder burn; the gun had gone off that close to his ancient face.

His heel caught on a step and he crashed into the dust. Calmly, Molly put one bullet an inch from his foot and another a half inch from his backside. Harvey the trapper went up in the air like a hen squatting on hot rocks, and took off across the street at speed, much to the delight of the onlookers.

Molly Floyd was cleaning her six-gun sometime later when she heard hoofbeats and looked up to see the man she had been waiting for, riding in on a travel-stained horse.

Birch had never looked so good, even though she quickly sensed he was not the same man she had left on the High Plains.

Molly Floyd awoke to find herself alone. Sitting up sharply in the big rumpled bed, she glimpsed the broad-shouldered silhouette of her lover standing on the balcony of their second-floor room, the crimson backwash of the dawn before him.

For a moment, her face clouded. Last night had been good, yet different from what she had anticipated. Birch was pleased to see her, sure, but something was not the same as before.

'Birch. . . ?'

He was lost in thought and did not move. Cigarette smoke trailed from his lips and wafted over the street on the morning breeze. The town was quiet, with only the yapping of a solitary dog breaking the stillness.

Molly pulled on her robe and padded barefoot onto the balcony, the boards cool and clean beneath her feet.

She touched his elbow and he turned to her, his face filled with shadows.

She asked tenderly, 'What is it, Birch?'

'Huh,' he shrugged, lost in thought.

'Something is wrong. I can see it on your face. I can feel it,' she explained. Her concern for him was genuine.

'Nothing is wrong. I am just beat, is all. It was a long ride from the valley, baby,' he answered, knowing she knew better.

Her eyes scanned his face. She knew him so well, yet had always been aware that there was a part of himself he kept hidden from her. He had told her little about his visit back home, other than he had seen his mother and 'kicked a mongrel dog' – whatever that might have meant.

101

'Did you find your mother well, Birch?' she prompted, eager to hear his answer.

'Her health has failed a lot, but I guess she is fine.' Birch looked at the crimson orb of the rising sun. 'She is married again.'

The last part caught her by surprise. 'Oh . . . is she happy then?'

It was not her fault that she did not know his history and about Bruce Gentry, Birch told himself.

'Who knows? What would I know about marriage?' His answer was a bit harsh, harsher than he expected.

Molly Floyd smiled roguishly. 'There is one good way to find out, lover.'

He looked at her first, and then they laughed together and with an arm around her waist, they watched the sun float clear off the plains before they went inside to dress for breakfast.

The eatery was a popular meeting place in the town, and the cowboys, teamers, miners and loafers who had assembled there to attack the pancakes and maple syrup, darted envious glances at the man seated at the corner table with the mystery lady.

Molly Floyd attracted attention everywhere she went, and this was even more apparent in this tiny, remote trail town, where plain women were at a premium and pretty ones were nonexistent. She had been the object of intense interest and speculation ever since her arrival several days earlier, and all the eligible bachelors, having made a play for her and been rejected, were keenly interested in her breakfast companion.

A traveling drummer thought Birch Kent looked vaguely familiar but could not place his face. The man had seen a Wanted poster tacked to a tree a long way north the previous week, but did not make the connection.

'Looks tough enough,' observed the town's bearded patriarch.

'And she is loco about him,' said another man, who looked to not have bathed in weeks. 'A blind man could see that fact.'

Heads all around him nodded in agreement. They might be rubes, but they were sophisticated enough to recognize a woman in love. They envied the stranger with the broad shoulders and only hoped he appreciated what he had in Molly. The patriarch advanced the view that this might not be the case. It seemed to him that the stranger's thoughts were someplace else.

'That must mean he is loco,' opined Harvey the trapper, who would love her till he died, despite the finality of her rejection. 'A beauty like her . . they don't come 'round these parts much. . . .'

'More than likely,' intoned the patriarch 'More than likely he is very crazy, Harvey.'

Birch used his fork to toy with his food, as unaware of the interest they were creating as he was of his companion's searching glances. His thoughts were back in the Valley of the Sun with his mother and Andrea. He had not planned on things going the way they had, yet upon reflection, he knew it had probably been inevitable. He regretted having upset their ordered lives on Alpha and in Painted River. But he did not in the least regret his confrontation with Gentry.

A smile touched his mouth as he gazed into the street. He could still feel the electric thrill that had coursed through his body as he had discovered with that one vicious cut with the whip, and in his mind's eye, could see the shirt leaping off Gentry's body, blood spraying in the air and his expression of excruciating agony.

Now the son of a bitch knew what it felt like!

Molly was forced to speak his name three times before he heard her. 'Sorry, baby. Maybe I am more beat than I thought,' he said.

'What are we going to do, Birch?' she asked eagerly.

'About what?' He was afraid she wanted to talk about them, and why he had changed. He could not explain about Andrea. How did you tell a woman who loved you that you were hopelessly in love with somebody else? He squeezed her hand and forced a grin. He loved Molly, but had always known he was not in love with her. If this was true, an inner voice suggested, he might as well settle for it, for Andrea was now, and always would be, out of the reach of this outlaw.

'I want to know if we are staying here or moving on?' Molly replied, to his relief.

Birch speared a pancake with his fork and surveyed the town's main stem. He had ridden through this place in the middle of a snowy night six years or so earlier, dodging lawmen, bounty hunters and one irate husband. He had never forgotten it. This small town in Nevada had struck him then as the ideal place for a man to hole up. Far from the main trails, with no law office and few strangers passing through, it was a haven for ruffians, hellions and saddle tramps. He liked it, and he did feel kind of weary.

'Want to stay a spell?' he threw out.

'I want to do anything you want, Birch.' Her reply was heartfelt and honest.

He leaned across the table and kissed her, almost bringing tears of envy to the eyes of their male audience.

'We have earned a break,' her outlaw lover said. 'I have got enough cash to see us through a week, maybe ten days. Then we will have to think about going back to work.'

Molly's eyes shone. 'Sounds wonderful, just the two of us in this sleepy little town. Maybe it will bring us closer, Birch.'

He evaded that one. 'Come on, finish up. I have got to get a letter away to my mother telling her I am okay. She will be worried about me.'

'All right. I would love to meet Adeline someday.'

'Sure, sure,' Birch Kent said. But he did not truly mean it. Molly Floyd would never get to meet Adeline Kent, because he would not be going back there himself. His first visit in a decade had almost ended in disaster. He knew he could not trust himself in Bruce Gentry's company. Next time he might kill the bastard, and that would not be right. He might never understand what had prompted Adeline to marry Big Bruce, but he was her husband now and Birch did not want to make her a widow again, tempting as the notion sounded to him.

He rose, feeling in his pocket for cash. 'We will go back someday. Ma will kill the fatted calf and we will have us a prodigal son party to celebrate. Let's go, baby.'

Harvey the trapper groaned aloud as Molly passed close to his chair, leaving behind a hint of perfume and a lasting impression of total desirability. She heard it and only hoped that Birch had not, as she did not want any trouble here. Fortunately, he appeared to not have heard the trapper.

'I gotta get back to the hills,' Harvey lamented. 'I will go loco here in the big city with all this temptation around.' He could barely take his eyes from Molly.

Nobody heard or cared to listen to the old mountain trapper. The others were all preoccupied with watching the broad-shouldered man and long-legged woman heading, arm-in-arm, for the post office. Such was life for Harvey Lyles, the trapper. He at times felt invisible.

The trail led downhill for a half mile or so, winding through the unnamed village at the eastern end of the Valley of the Sun. The rider patted the horse's sweaty neck. Beneath his fingers, veins stood out like ropes under the animal's tightly-drawn skin. It was played out, but that did not matter now, for they were close to their destination.

He passed through the village, the houses and shacks thinning out as he continued westward. Some of the villagers had recognized him and a few had shouted a greeting. The rider had not paused; he was heading for Painted River.

The creek came into view, looking like a sleepy, brown snake, always moving. The horse's hoofs echoed hollowly as they crossed the bridge.

When he saw the double strands of barbed wire fence running west, the rider knew he was on the Barber Ranch, the valley's second biggest. The barbed wire extended all the way into Painted River, where the large Alpha Ranch took over, filling the entire western arm of the valley.

The rider knew every fence, canyon and blade of grass in the Valley of the Sun. He also knew most of its people, although it had been a long time since he had worn the five-pointed star on Painted River's streets.

'Hello there, Sheriff!' a man bellowed as he entered the town from the east. 'Vacation time again, huh?'

Rigdon Elliott nodded without a word. They still called him 'Sheriff' in these parts, even though he had not been the law in the town for many years; he was now a Federal Marshal. He had not allowed them to forget him in the valley, returning as he did every year for his vacation, or occasionally stopping over in the hunt for some outlaw or other. Always a popular figure here, Elliott was well-received every time he came back, and the locals liked to believe he enjoyed the valley so much he just could not stay away.

They were wrong, of course. He had an entirely different reason for coming back. It was a reason that would draw him as long as he lived.

A reason that only he and one other knew.

CHAPTER 9

PAIN AND SECRETS

The doctor, a man in his late fifties, examined the bottle of pills on the wooden bureau; it was almost full he noted. He shook his head as he made for the door.

'What's the point, Mr Gentry? I don't know how you expect to recover if you don't take the medication I recommend, Mr Gentry,' he scolded the ranch owner.

'What are you talking about, doc? You just said I am healing as fast as anybody you ever saw,' Bruce Gentry shot back. A cough followed his response. He grimaced some with the cough.

'You would heal a hell of a lot quicker if you took the medicine,' the doctor noted sternly.

'I take it every day,' Big Bruce fired back. He

grabbed the bottle of whiskey standing on the bedside table and uncorked it. 'Every day,' he emphasized, and took a slug that would have stunned a buffalo.

Shaking his head, the medical doctor made his way to the sunlit front gallery of the house, where the two lovely ladies of the house – Adeline and Bruce's niece, Andrea – sat at a small rattan table, drinking coffee.

'How is he, Doctor?' Adeline asked perfunctorily.

'Healthier than I am,' the doctor replied, coughing. He was a heavy smoker and had been for most of his adult life. 'Not that that is sayin' so much, I guess. Your husband has a remarkable constitution, Mrs Gentry. I wish you shared some of it. Would you like to have me check you over while I am here?'

Adeline shook her head. 'I am sick of doctors, Doctor.' She then shot him a quick look of embarrassment, adding, 'No offense.'

'I guess I can appreciate that, ma'am.' The doctor cleared his throat and swallowed hard, 'Er, I don't suppose anyone feels like tellin' me how Mr Gentry came by that injury, or who creased his hand, Mr Legler, huh?'

He was right. Nobody felt a bit like it at the moment. It was just another thing he, as a doctor, could not fix, people swallowing their tongues as it were – keeping the truth to themselves.

The doctor left, shaking his head and coughing still. He could live with unsatisfied curiosity. Bruce Gentry always paid promptly and paid well, which was about all that really concerned him. They were welcome to their secrets – just as long as he got his money, he did not press the matter further.

The women watched him leave. Nobody outside Alpha Ranch was aware of Birch's recent visit. Big Bruce had insisted on silence. The return of his illegitimate son was not something he wanted broadcast to the four winds. He had a reputation to uphold, an image that could not help but be damaged by a lurid story of his bastard son's violent visit.

That did not mean the affair had been forgotten. Anything but. Adeline firmly believed the prime factor in her husband's recovery from that terrible whip stroke, was hate. Big Bruce Gentry had always hated Birch because he knew Adeline loved her son in a way she would never care for him. And this incident had added fuel to the fire, and to his hatred of Birch.

This was the second-time Birch had bested Big Bruce and gotten away with it. Adeline did not know what steps her husband would take to track Birch down; she only knew he would not just let it lie. Not now. The father-son feud had gone too far. How it would end, nobody knew, but Adeline Gentry coped by staying calm.

'More coffee, dear?' she asked Andrea.

Andrea Gentry looked wan and had done so ever since Birch's visit. 'No, thanks, Adeline. When do you expect to hear from Birch?'

'Soon, I reckon,' Adeline Gentry replied, sipping her coffee, trying to be hopeful. 'He writes often.'

'I have to know he is all right,' Andrea said, a tad sheepishly.

Adeline's gray eyes shadowed as she studied the lovely woman seated opposite. She had always suspected that Andrea cared for her son, and now she was certain that she did. When Birch and Andrea were together, their mutual attraction was obvious. Adeline could understand it, but did not approve. All she could envision for any woman who might fall in love with her son, was heartbreak.

'Have faith in Birch,' Adeline said. 'I have always believed nothing could really hurt that boy after what he survived nearly ten years ago. . . .'

Adeline's voice trailed away as the sound of boots crunching on gravel announced the arrival of Hugh Legler. The big bodyguard carried his left arm in a sling and his complexion was yellow. The doctor said Legler's wound was not half as serious as Gentry's, yet the younger man was much slower to recover. Not enough hate, maybe, Adeline speculated.

Legler halted at the steps. 'Mr Gentry about, ladies?'

'In the front room,' Adeline supplied. 'How is the shoulder today, Mr Legler?'

The big man nodded as he spoke. 'Healing, ma'am.'

Legler vanished inside and Andrea sighed. 'I wish it had been different, Adeline. I wish there hadn't been violence. Perhaps Birch may have stayed on. Do you think he would have?'

'No. His father would always stand in his way.'

Adeline was direct and cold in her response.

'I can't help being puzzled, Adeline . . . I mean, I know how you love Birch, yet you married his father, who hates him. I realize it is none of my business, but I could never understand your marrying Uncle Bruce after Aunt Laura passed away, even though I knew you had always been . . . close.'

In that moment of close companionship, Adeline Gentry suddenly realized, with a small sense of surprise, something she had always suspected, which was that Andrea was trustworthy. The girl was as reliable as the sunrise, hated Big Bruce, loved her son, and had always proved herself to be a true friend.

Adeline decided it was now safe to confide in Andrea. It was something she had always wanted to be able to do, but had held back because of her concern for her son's safety.

Birch had always been the most important person on earth to her and always would be.

'Honey,' she said, 'what do you know about Laura's will?'

Andrea Gentry looked surprised. 'Why, very little, I'm afraid. But why do you ask?'

'You knew she left half of Alpha Ranch to me, didn't you?'

Andrea's smile was wry. 'It would have been impossible not to know, Adeline, the way Uncle Bruce carried on at the time.'

'Have you ever wondered why Laura did that?' Adeline asked.

'I assumed that it was because you were close

friends?' Andrea offered.

'That was only part of the reason. You see, honey, Laura always knew about Bruce and me. At first she was angry, and I don't blame her for being that way. But when Birch came along, she changed. They could never have children, Laura and Bruce, and Laura was desperate for a family. Birch became her surrogate son. She adored him, Andrea, and it seemed the more Bruce hated him, the more Laura loved him. What happened here all those years ago that drove Birch from the valley was the worst part of Laura's life. She never forgot Birch and insisted on reading every letter I received. She grew to hate Bruce for what he had done to him. I think she hated him even more than I do.'

Andrea was stunned.

'You hate Uncle Bruce? But why then did you marry him?'

'For Birch.' Adeline's face became cold and resolute. 'You see, Andrea, although I was never proud of my relationship with Big Bruce, I really had little choice. It was a case of allowing him to share my bed, or starving. I chose the former, and was reasonably content before he drove Birch away. I always had this secret dream of Birch inheriting Alpha, through Bruce. And when I was left half the ranch, and Bruce proposed in the hope of cheating me out of my share, I accepted for one reason and one reason only; I intend to outlive my husband and turn over the entire Alpha Ranch to my son. It is his birthright.'

114

*

Big Bruce Gentry growled angrily, 'Hand me my shirt. '

Hugh Legler obliged. Gentry went to the mirror to check the strapping on his chest and back before donning his shirt. The whip had caught him across the left pectoral, cut into the deltoid muscle of the shoulder then carved a fifteen-inch channel across his back, reaching almost to the waist.

He winced a little as he struggled into his shirt, but had no difficulty in buttoning it. Whiskey and hate really were a good combination for recovery, he had discovered. He had plenty of both.

'So, what news?' he demanded as he tucked the shirt in around his hard, flat waist.

'So far, nothin'.' Wise and Legler oversaw the manhunt. Big Bruce now wanted his son dead and did not care how much it cost, or how long it took. He had fifteen high-class bounty hunters on his payroll for this operation; it would be time enough to tell her when Birch was in the ground. Legler was as eager to see that day as his employer, but it was beginning to appear that Birch would not be easily taken.

Gentry led the way out into the yard, ignoring the women on the gallery. His step was vigorous, his color high. The whip, his best friend, was now coiled over his shoulder. It hurt, but he would not be without it. It was the same whip he had used on his son some ten years earlier. Having tasted its

115

murderous bite, he had an even keener apprecia-
tion of what it could do. He dreamed of Birch
being taken alive so he could finish him off with
the whip. Should such an opportunity arise, it
would have to be handled secretly, of course. He
would see Adeline's son dead, but she would not
know who had killed him. Big Bruce had always
believed that the frail Adeline would die first and
leave her half of Alpha Ranch to him, which would
see him become sole owner after what seemed like
an eternity.

He hated women for what they had put him
through over this land, but would acknowledge only
to himself that without them, Big Bruce Gentry
would probably still be just a fortune-hunting
nobody.

At the corrals, he jerked off his shirt again to allow
the sun to get at his body; he realized this hastened
the healing process. He was still sunbathing and discussing the manhunt with Legler, when the marshal
arrived.

Leaning on a railing, watching Elliott dismount,
Gentry saw Adeline rush out to welcome the lawman
and his lip curled.

For nearly twenty years, Gentry had suspected
Adeline was in love with Rigdon Elliott and vice
versa. It no longer bothered him. He had given up
trying to command first place in her heart long ago
when he had realized it was their son she loved and
not him. This had been the breeding ground for his
sick hatred of Birch Kent. Elliott, he could take, for

the lawman was nothing if not discreet. Gentry was sure his association with Adeline was platonic; Elliott would have died with a bullet in the back had he thought otherwise.

'Too bad we can't make use of him, boss,' Legler said. 'Elliott was always the best in the business when it came to runnin' people down.'

Big Bruce, who had no knowledge of his son's outlaw career, shook his head. 'Not him. He would be no use to us. Why, when the bastard shot Felder, Elliott refused to enter it in the books as murder. Instead, he threatened to take action against me for attempting to murder him. . . .'

They were interrupted by the arrival of Wise. Watching the man spurring his horse towards them, the brooding Gentry suddenly straightened, realizing Wise looked excited.

He was right; Wise was elated. He had just collected a letter for Adeline at the post office. It was in Birch's handwriting and the postmark was Nevada.

'We got the son of a bitch now!' Bruce Gentry breathed. 'Legler, who is closest to Nevada?'

Hugh Legler had to consult his notebook dealing with the whereabouts of their various bands of bounty hunters before supplying the name, 'Hedgepeth'. 'He was in southwest Utah headin' for Las Vegas at last report, boss. . . .'

'How many men with him?' Gentry demanded.

'Um . . . looks to be five,' Legler answered.

'That won't be enough. Who is near him to help out?' Gentry felt his heart racing now.

117

The answer came up; Mort Haggins and a few men in northern Arizona.

'Wire them directly to meet up with Hedgepeth at Las Vegas,' Big Bruce Gentry ordered, his eyes flashing with excitement. 'Tell them there is an extra thousand dollars in bonus per man if they reach Nevada in time and that they are all fired if they don't.'

An hour later, Adeline Gentry was reading her warm, loving letter from her son while the telegraph lines stretching from Painted River hummed with messages authorizing his destruction.

And in the next room, her husband sipped whiskey with Marshal Rigdon Elliott and deplored the West's lawlessness.

CHAPTER 10

BIG KILL IN HUACHUA HILLS

'Mornin', Birch,' Molly Floyd said.

'Morning,' he replied, almost automatically.

'Cleaning your Colt, huh?' she probed him.

He didn't flinch or move, other than the cleaning he was doing. 'Looks to be the case.'

'Figurin' on doin' some shootin' soon?' she asked, already knowing the answer.

Birch raised his pistol and sighted it squarely on Harvey the trapper's skinny chest. 'Reckon that could be the case.'

Harvey the trapper vanished down the boardwalk at speed, raising little clouds of dust with his big boots.

Birch Kent half-grinned. Everyone knew why the trapper was still in town. Harvey had a king-sized crush on Molly. She treated him like dirt and he had developed a healthy fear of Birch, yet he lingered on in Huachua Hills, on the Nevada–Arizona border, in the desperate hope that things might somehow change and he would yet get to win his heart's desire.

'Hope blooms eternal. . . .' Birch mused and returned to his chore, tilting his chair back against the hotel wall, until the toes of his boots just touched the floorboards.

He forced the oily rag through the pistol with the cleaning rod, then held the muzzle to his eye to peer down the gleaming barrel.

Clean as a preacher's soul, he told himself.

He tested the action and was reloading the weapon when he looked up to see the town patriarch watching him intently from a porch across the street.

Birch Kent waved and the graybeard waved back. They liked him, he knew, but at the same time, he detected a hint of wariness. A big, healthy man as he was, with no visible means of support, hanging around with a beautiful woman who was tough enough to scare just about everybody in town when she put her mind to it, was a matter of some concern to the citizens of the small town of Huachua Hills.

Birch deliberately executed a fast draw, and the patriarch almost fell off his stool in fright.

'It is all right,' Birch called. 'Just practising . . . just practising.'

He shouldn't have done that, he chided himself as the old man vanished indoors with wings on his heels. He supposed it was a sign of boredom. Peace and tranquility were all very well, but in time, they could lose their novelty and make a man yearn for a little honest-to-God excitement.

Birch flexed his arms, stretched his legs and stared off at nothing. He was thinking of the valley. He rarely thought of anything else these days. Going back had been a big mistake, even though he had been desperate to see his mother and Andrea. The visit had only served to remind him how badly he missed the old life, while the realization that Andrea was still in love with him after so many years was both exhilarating and depressing. He loved her too, but could never have her.

What was so great about that?

From beneath his tilted hat brim, he sighted Molly emerging from a store on the town's main street and walking across the street. Dressed in a dark, most likely black, blouse and moleskins, she moved with the flowing grace of a wild creature, like somebody who had first learned to walk on crisp mountain mornings, with the wind in her face and the whole world fresh and bright around her.

His woman. Perhaps one of the only people in the world who cared for him despite knowing who he was.

Birch was both proud and sad at that though, proud that Molly was his, sad that he could never love her the way she deserved.

Only for her, he would still be rotting away in Yuma Territorial Prison, he chided himself. Nobody but Molly could have planned and executed his

121

escape the way she had. She was a better partner than any man he had ever ridden with, loyal and dedicated. He should love her, but a fragile, unattainable girl with eyes of emerald held him fast.

When Molly stopped to speak to a town matron, Birch allowed his gaze to drift. Dust rose above the trail; someone was coming into town. Snow-capped mountains floated in the hazy distance like the mysterious spires of another world.

He realized that the peace had soaked into him so deeply, the hate that had been revitalized back in Painted River seemed to be dwindling.

He shoved his hand into his pocket and dragged out some bills. Not much left. It would soon be time to start work again.

A shadow fell across him and he looked up into Molly's face.

'Daydreaming again, baby?' She grinned. 'That is getting to be a habit with you, isn't it?'

'I was just thinking about Yuma,' he grinned. 'Those long, lazy days on the rockpile, guessing if the meat was polecat or snake, my pet rat in the hole named James, those swell times we stood in the stock yards at attention all day in the heat because a bottle was found in somebody's cell. . . . Ah, those were the days, Molly.'

'Speaking of bottles,' Molly smiled, and was hauling a flash of scotch from her pocket when a bunch of kids went by at the run, making for the Mexico border.

'Hey, what is going on?' Birch called.

'Medicine show,' called a skinny kid with ginger hair and huge freckles. 'Come take a gander!'

'Well, you heard him.' Birch chuckled, getting up. 'This could be the most excitement we will see in this town, baby.'

'Only hope my heart can stand all the excitement.' His sarcasm was not lost on Molly.

A small crowd had already gathered as the gaudily colorful horse-drawn van of Dr Simmons' Traveling Medicine Show halted before the store and immediately went into action. The horses were unharnessed, a small stage attached to the van's tailgate, then a bearded man played the harmonica very badly as a salesman wearing a bulging yellow waistcoat and silk topper mounted the stage to launch into his spiel.

'Lady and gentlemen, thank you for your wonderful warm welcome and allow me to introduce myself. I have the honor to be the distinguished Dr Simmons of the Boston Medical School who has journeyed two-thirds of the way across this continent to bring you what every man, woman and child amongst you has been waiting for all their lives.' The harmonica played a fanfare as the 'doctor' whipped out a bottle from an inside pocket.

'This,' the man said with flamboyant flair.

'This' turned out to be Dr Simmons' Wonder Liver Elixir and Purgative at a dollar a bottle. According to its purveyor, the elixir would cure anything from halitosis to frigidity in women and inadequacy in men.

'That is all well and good,' a familiar voice

123

hollered, and Birch and Molly saw Harvey the trapper elbowing his way to the fore. 'But is it a love potion? That is what I want to know.'

There was general laughter, for everyone knew of the trapper's infatuation for Molly Floyd.

'Love potion, sir?' boomed the salesman, holding the bottle high. 'My dear fellow, a slug of this would make a bobcat fall for a grizzly bear. Of course, it is a love potion, the greatest known to medical science!'

He was good, this joker, Birch thought. Then, as the man leaned forward to exchange a bottle of sugared water for a one-dollar bill, Birch wondered why he was watching him from the corner of his eye.

Birch Kent had only that split second of warning there was something odd about Dr Simmons' Traveling Medicine Show before the side of the van fell away and he was confronted by a row of gunmen.

Responding with the speed of lightning, Birch's left arm swept Molly to the ground as his right hand came up with his roaring pistol.

The thunder of Birch's pistol was enhanced by the bloodcurdling roar of the bounty hunters' guns, and the tiny town was filled with the screams of terror as a bounty hunter, a child, and unlucky Harvey the trapper all fell in that first mad exchange of hot lead.

The seconds blurred for Birch as he realized every man in the van, including the 'doctor' and his harmonica player, was gunning for him. Hurling his body sideways, he fanned his gun hammer and another man spilled from the van to smash face-first into the ground with a hole above his right ear.

Then Birch was hit. The bullet raked his arm, and his pistol dropped to the ground with a thud. As he scrambled for it, he knew he had no chance. They had to get him.

And they would have, but for Molly. Suddenly, she was there, protecting him from the hungry guns with her own slim body, the .38 which she handled so expertly snarling in her hand, spewing fire and smoke.

'Molly, get down!' he screamed.

Birch's cry was lost in the totality of deafening sound. He saw a bounty hunter clutch at his guts and sag at the knees moments before Molly was knocked backwards under the impact of driving lead. She crashed across Birch's body just as his hand closed over his gun.

Horrified, Birch stared into her eyes and saw them already glazing over as she breathed his name and then died.

He took a bullet in the chest as he surged up on one knee, but it would have required a cannon ball to stop him now. Left palm fanning his gun hammer, he emptied his pistol into the van, then snatched up Molly's .38 and drilled a soft-nosed slug squarely in the 'doctor's' left eye, spattering his brains all over the sign advertising the Wonder Elixir.

Suddenly, the killers who had plotted their ambush so carefully were looking like losers, out-gunned by a female and a man who was vastly more lethal than they had been led to believe. This bastard they had come to kill was sudden death on two feet.

When Birch drove a bullet squarely through the back of the harmonica player to drop him in a bloodied heap, the three survivors took to their heels, running from the chaos of Southwestern Arizona into the crooked street that led to the river.

Looking like a crazed man, with blood soaking his shirtfront from his own and Molly's wounds, Birch went after them, reloading from his belt as he ran. He glimpsed bobbing heads over a fence, but held his fire as he lengthened his stride. He would not waste gunpowder. He wanted three butchers dead at his feet and would get them or die trying.

When he reached the rim of the creek, Birch flattened himself on the ground and parted the shrubbery to look down. He saw nothing. They had gone to ground.

In the background, he heard wailing and weeping. It took a particular breed of butcher to open up on a crowd containing women and children, he thought grimly.

He felt around until he found a rock which he pitched high over the creek bed. It struck with a clatter and a slim figure in a dark shirt bobbed up from a screen of brush on the right and fired two quick shots.

Birch shot the man twice in the head and once in the guts as he fell.

Rolling back from the edge as lead stormed about him, Birch refilled the pistol. He waited. Soon the guns fell silent and a man's hoarse voice shouted, 'Let's parley, Birch. We don't want you this bad, man.'

126

Birch Kent was bleeding and breathing hard as he slithered soundlessly through prickly leaves and stiff twigs of holly oak. He was moving towards the river, figuring that would be the direction they would take if they retreated, and he expected them to do just that – he expected them to run like the cowards there were! His heart ached for Molly and the dead town-folk all over the streets. There was a leaden taste in his mouth and his throat was as dry as prairie dust.

A stone clicked in the creek bed. Birch used his gun barrel to part some branches and squinted down to see a blocky, thick-waisted man wearing a sourdough jacket and a coonskin cap, climbing over a boulder.

'This is for her,' he called, and as the bounty hunter twisted, he shot him through the throat. The man clutched at his throat and could be heard attempting to scream but it came out only as a bloody gurgle.

Birch jumped to his feet as he sighted movement farther down the creek. He was as ruthless and murderous as a scalp-hunting Apache as he gave chase, dimly aware in the far recesses of his brain that, at least, this was staving off his grief and sense of guilt. 'The cure for grief,' an inner voice said cynically, 'is killing more.'

Birch told the voice to shut up and hurried along the creek bed with his gun cocked and his every sense honed razor-sharp. He wanted to meet the last man fast and get it over with. But he was not careless;

he placed his feet with care and stifled the sound of his breathing.

He was leaving crimson splotches on the hot stones behind him.

He watched the rocks and brush on either side. The bounty man was still ahead of him, unless he had pulled a Birch Kent trick and climbed the walls of the creek to double back.

So, he had to watch the ground, the creek walls, the route ahead and his backtrail all at once, which was the sort of task you needed about four sets of eyes to handle properly. His head and eyes were moving constantly, staying vigilant.

Then the tracks in the dust simply stopped, and Birch realized his quarry had seized an overhanging branch and swung himself up out of the bed and on to the bank.

Birch followed suit, his breath tearing in his lungs from the exertion. His head swam as he dropped to one knee in a patch of undergrowth to regain his breath. His heart hammered and he was not seeing clearly. He had lost too much blood, and was losing more. If he did not run this bastard down fast, he would not run him down at all. He would pass out from loss of blood first.

A gun roared and a bullet creased his shoulder as, from the corner of his eye, he sighted the crouched figure behind a dead tree. Birch fell on his back and fired backwards behind his head, blasting off three shots to confuse the gunman. Then he flipped back on to his knees, saw the bounty hunter darting away and fired again, but not for effect. This time, the shot was meant to kill and only failed to do so by an inch as the running man, struck high in the chest, spun and fell.

Feeling a hundred years old, Birch Kent somehow lurched erect and staggered forward.

The downed bounty hunter was sprawled in a thicket of blue thorn and was hurting again, but his aim was erratic. He was badly wounded, yet still dangerous.

Birch was not quite sure how much of a danger he himself posed, but his legs kept carrying him onwards over shale and weeds.

The bounty hunter stayed down, coughing blood and cursing as he squeezed the trigger again, only to hear the hollow click of the hammer on an empty shell.

Birch loomed over the dying man, gun leveled. There was no suggestion of pity in his cold eyes, nothing but iron in the set of his jaw and the tightness of his mouth.

'Don't do it,' the man pleaded.

'Why not?' Birch could feel the earth swaying beneath his feet. 'Give me one good reason not to.'

'Well . . . well, we didn't get you, did we?' the man tried to rationalize.

'You got my lady, scumbag,' Birch said through clenched teeth.

The man clawed at Birch's pants leg. 'I will give you anythin', do anythin' for you! For heaven's sake!'

Birch wondered dully why he had not fired yet.

Then he realized that his brain was working so sluggishly, the obvious question had taken twice as long as normal to get through.

'Who hired you?' Birch demanded. 'The law?'

'If I tell you,' the bounty hunter began. 'Will you let me live?'

Birch could see the man was dying. His bullet may have missed the heart, but only by a whisker. He was losing blood rapidly and it would not be long before he was standing at the gates of hell.

'Sure,' Birch grunted. 'Who hired you?'

The man sleeved his mouth and gasped, 'You know a big bastard named Gentry?'

CHAPTER 11

UNREQUITED LOVE

The sun was like a ball of fire on Birch's back. His head throbbed like a drum and the beat of his heart pulsing in his ears was erratic. He spat, tasting dirt, and realized he had fallen in a ploughed field. Long lines of yellow corn surrounded him, heads nodded in the sun.

Birch shook his head. He had been whipped by Big Bruce Gentry. He was under the Joshua tree and they were coming for him. He could hear the crunch of boots and the barking of dogs . . . He had to move, get running! Gentry would hang him; he knew it . . . He did not want to die at sixteen; he just wanted to live long enough to run a fully loaded Colt into that big bastard's guts and give him six slugs at close range. . . . His head spun and darkness claimed him.

It was dusk when he awoke to find he was still lying in the Nevadan corn field with a bullet in the chest and fire in his throat.

He was alive!

That knowledge surprised him. He examined his chest and saw that the blood had congealed and the bleeding had stopped. He groaned and rested the palms of his hands on the ground and pushed himself to his feet. Somehow, he remained vertical. He felt terrible, but not as weak as he had been.

His mind was clear and he remembered everything.

When the thefts were discovered the next morning, the citizens of Huachua Hills did not relate the incident to Birch Kent. His disappearance and the bloody trail he had left convinced them he was dead, and that a surviving bounty hunter had probably returned to rob them in the dead of night.

When county lawmen arrived to conduct an investigation into the bloodbath, they kept hearing the name 'Birch' and finally came up with a description that matched the escapee from Yuma Territorial Prison, Birch Hamilton. After hearing all reports on the outlaw, last seen pursuing three bounty hunters with a bullet hole in his chest, they were also ready to proclaim him dead.

The papers gave great prominence to the 'Huachua Hills Massacre' and if there was anybody west of the Mississippi River who was aware that the notorious gang leader, Birch Hamilton, had cashed in his chips, was dead as a wagon wheel, along with his paramour, the beautiful, infamous, and deadly Molly Floyd, it was not their fault.

Although Painted River's physician was a pessimist by nature and always ready to predict the worst possible outcome for any malady, he did not exaggerate when he announced that Adeline Gentry was dying. She had never been strong, and he had watched her steadily decline throughout her marriage to Big Bruce Gentry. But it was the news of her son's death that brought her to her sick bed, and as the doctor told Andrea that sodden day that heralded the beginning of a week's rain, he did not expect her to recover this time.

'She has given up, Miss Andrea. It is as simple as that. Do you know why?' the doctor asked.

Andrea Gentry shook her head. Nobody outside Alpha Ranch knew that Birch Kent and the outlaw Birch Hamilton were one and the same, and both Big Bruce and Adeline insisted that secret be preserved.

'I have no idea, Doctor,' Andrea said sheepishly. She was not a fan of lying, no matter how good the reason behind the lie was. 'But surely you can do something for Adeline?'

'Once a person quits on life, I am afraid that is it . . .' The medico bent a dark stare on the familiar figure striding across the house yard. 'And I have a strong suspicion Mr Gentry is not helping the situation.'

Andrea's face was cold with hatred as she watched her uncle approach. She knew that Big Bruce had been pestering Adeline to change her will ever since she had taken ill. He wanted her to make him the beneficiary, not Birch. It was as callous and cold-hearted a thing as Andrea had ever known him to do, but she was hardly surprised. She was convinced there was very little Big Bruce Gentry could not or would not do to achieve his own ends or indulge his own passions.

Gentry halted on the steps. 'What is the verdict today, Doc?'

The doctor hesitated before replying. There was no way to sugar coat the response. 'Your wife is weaker, Mr Gentry.'

'That is awful,' Big Bruce muttered, going in. 'Yes, that is too bad. Oh yes, that is just too damn bad. . . .'

'I wish he would leave Mrs Gentry alone, Miss Andrea,' the doctor said softly. 'Every time he sees her, she seems to slip back even farther. It is like his presence harms her.'

'It isn't fair, is it, Doctor?' Andrea said with sudden spirit. 'Life, I mean. Here we have a lovely, kind woman who has never done anything but good in her life, dying from grief, while her husband, whom half the valley would like to see in his grave, only seems to grow stronger and healthier every day.'

The doctor was shocked. 'Why, Miss Andrea, I have never heard you speak about Mr Gentry that way!'

'He is a monster,' Andrea retorted, and strode away, leaving the medico stroking his jaw and looking

134

very tired, while inside the great house, in a room filled with flowers, the 'monster' was living up to the tag Andrea had given him.

'I am not accepting a refusal today,' Big Bruce growled, holding the papers before Adeline's pale face. 'You are going to change this damn will today, and I won't leave this room until you do.'

'That is all you married me for, isn't it, Bruce? To try and get back the land Laura left me?' Adeline said with a weak voice.

'I am not here to talk, woman.' Big Bruce wore a look of disgust on his face. 'Are you going to sign this, or aren't you?'

Adeline mustered all the strength she could to look at her husband with spite. 'Never. When I die, Birch will inherit my half of Alpha Ranch. It is his birthright!'

'Don't give me that hogwash. That bastard coming into this world was an accident and we both know it. He has got no more rights than any other bastard. Ask any attorney and you will hear the same thing,' Big Bruce said.

Adeline looked at the rain streaming down her windows. 'The happiest accident of my life. . . .'

Gentry began pacing to and fro, showing no after-effects of his injury now. He was restored to full vigor.

'Now look, dammit, all this talk about your son is academic, madam. He is dead. He can't inherit anything, and all I am asking you to do is sign these papers, so there won't be any hitches if, heaven forbid, something should happen to you.' He tried to sound sincere, he failed.

His greed and callous indifference were so patently plain that Adeline was not affected. But she was puzzled.

'I know he is dead,' she said softly, 'but do you?'

Big Bruce Gentry jerked to a halt. 'What? What do you mean by that?'

'All this fuss about my will. I have spoken to the attorney and he has told me that if my son is dead, and in the absence of any codicil to the contrary, you would be able to make a claim on my legacy and win. But if that is the case, why are you badgering me so much about changing the will?'

'I have already told you, dammit. I just want to simplify . . .' he began.

'You don't believe that Birch is dead!' There was some excitement in her voice.

The blood drained from Big Bruce Gentry's broad face, and a nerve jumped in his cheek. Instantly, Adeline knew her barb had struck home. It was dead on target.

'You are crazy,' he said hoarsely. 'The papers are full of that gunfight in Nevada. You will never see that trouble-making bastard again, and good riddance I say. Now, about these papers. . . .'

She tried to push the papers away. 'Take them away, Bruce.'

Big Bruce Gentry loomed over the bed. 'Don't push me too far, Adeline. You are not in any position to force conditions or take stands, remember. You could end up dying in the poorhouse if it suited me. . . .'

'I doubt that, Mr Gentry.'

Gentry whirled. Rigdon Elliott stood in the doorway, hat in hand. The lawman's face was stony and he looked taller than Gentry remembered.

'Who the hell let you in?' the rancher snarled.

The marshal entered the room. Elliott nodded to Adeline and faced Gentry. 'I let myself in when I heard a raised voice. I am sure this sort of thing can't be good for your wife, Mr Gentry.'

Big Bruce bit his lower lip. Had he loved his wife, the lawman's obvious dedication to her would have been a constant irritant. But this was not the case, Gentry had always made a habit of treating Elliott with respect, a wise course of action with a man who wielded as much power and influence as the marshal.

Elliott's current visit to the valley was poorly timed as far as Gentry was concerned, but he kept his thoughts to himself. A clash with Elliott was the last thing he needed at the moment.

Even so, Bruce Gentry could not trust himself to speak, and merely gave a bad-tempered grunt as he strode out, banging the door behind him.

Adeline Gentry smiled as Rigdon Elliott took the chair by the bed. This quiet lawman was everything that Gentry had never been to her. They were in love, but had never been lovers. And now she could feel herself slipping away, she regretted the sacrifices she had had to make in order to preserve her son's inheritance.

Elliott had proposed to Adeline at the time Laura Gentry had passed away but she had feared that if she did not accept Gentry's proposal, he would find some way of cheating her out of her share of Alpha Ranch. Her rejection of Elliott had not affected their relationship. He still loved her. She only had to look at him to be sure of that.

'Any further news, Rigdon?' she asked hopefully.

'On Birch? No. They have not found the body.' He could not look her in the eyes as he responded.

Adeline sighed heavily. 'It is hard to believe he is gone.'

'Indeed, it is. I have never known a stronger man,' offered the lawman.

'You always liked him, didn't you, Rigdon?'

There was no hesitation from the lawman. 'Yes.'

'Do you know something?' she asked.

'What is that, Adeline?' Marshal Elliott prompted her.

'I have a feeling that when he escaped from prison, you did not really try to run him down,' she gave him a look that said she already knew the answer.

Rigdon Elliott crossed his legs and almost smiled. The woman was something, he mused. 'You know me too well, Adeline.' He sobered. 'From the very beginning, I saw Birch as a victim of circumstance. Before the incident with Gentry, he was a hard-working, straight-as-a-gun-barrel kind of lad, devoted to his mother and liked by everyone. Then his father almost killed him with a whip and hunted him like a wild animal, and he killed a man to save his own life. After that, he had no alternative but to go on the

138

dodge. Birch wasn't an outlaw by desire or design, Adeline, just a victim of blind circumstance. In truth, I always thought of him as a better man than most people I know.'

Adeline took his hand. 'I wish Birch was here to hear you speak that way, Rigdon.'

'I think he knew how I respected him,' admitted the lawman.

'Past tense, Rigdon?' she asked.

'Sorry.' He did not know what else to say.

'Is he dead, Rigdon? Do you really believe he is gone?' Tears welled in her eyes as she asked

'I only know one thing for certain, Adeline. He was an uncommonly hard man to kill.' That was no lie and that relieved Elliott.

He saw that helped Adeline. But as she drifted off to sleep, he knew it was not enough. Never strong, this recent sequence of events, culminating in the Nevada shootout, had drained her. The marshal was trying to resign himself to losing her, but it was the hardest thing he had ever done. He would surrender his career, his good name and everything he possessed if he thought it would help her recover.

However, he knew only one thing could give her the will to live and that was to see her son alive and well, and that would not happen.

CHAPTER 12

THE LAST DUEL

Big Bruce Gentry cursed the rain as he emerged from the Painted River jailhouse and went splashing across the street, slicker flapping, hat tugged low over his eyes. Frank Wise and Hugh Legler waited for him under the overhang of the general store, smoking cheroots. Main Street, Painted River, was already a yellow sea of mud, and the rain was getting heavier.

The weather was in keeping with Big Bruce's mood. He had just checked with the sheriff to learn there had been no further developments regarding Birch's presumed death. In other words, the Nevadan authorities had not located the corpse.

'He is alive,' Gentry said as he stood under the overhang brushing water off his shoulders with a gloved hand. The lines in his face were deeply etched as he stared along the street. 'Nobody's as hard to kill

140

as that scum; I should know that better than anybody.' He thumped his midriff with a clenched fist. 'I can feel it in my guts. He is out there some-place, licking his wounds and biding his time until he comes back to haunt me. Judas Priest, won't I ever be rid of that bastard?'

Legler pursed his lips. 'We have been talkin', boss.'

'About Birch,' Wisc affirmed, looking pleased with himself. 'We think we have figured out a way.'

'A way to do what?' Bruce Gentry was testy.

'To find out if he is dead or alive,' Legler supplied. 'You interested, boss?'

Big Bruce blinked at them. Of course he was inter-ested. And after they had finished telling him what they had in mind, he was astonished. He was not accustomed to hearing good ideas from his body-guards, but there was always a first time for everything.

Birch Kent's color was slowly changing from sallow to deep brown as he continued to soak up the south-western sun. The town's horse doctor stopped by the cantina to check up on his patient like clockwork every day. But now, all they mostly did was talk and have a couple of drinks. The patient was plainly recovering well.

'Until I met up with you, son,' the veterinarian said with his gravelly voice that day, 'I always thought the toughest critter I had ever struck was an army mule. But you . . . whew . . . you take the prize. What is your secret, son?'

'Clean living,' Birch replied. 'And no worries. Worry will kill a man quicker than any bullet.'

The doctor laughed at his patient and shook his head. 'I am serious, son.'

'So am I,' replied Birch.

The man sighed. 'Still won't tell me how you came by that bullet, I suppose?' The veterinarian had a look of hope on his face.

'My wife got mad at me when I told her I didn't like her speckled gravy. She is a woman with one hell of a temper. You think I am the toughest critter, huh.' Birch was somewhat believable in his story.

The vet gave up then. He finished his drink and left quietly. Birch leaned back in his chair and let the heat soak into him until his belly growled and he went inside to eat.

There was a newspaper on the counter and he noted idly that the so-called 'Battle of the Nevada Outlaw' had shifted back to the third page.

But there was an item at the bottom of the front page that caught his eye, as indeed it was meant to. It was a brief item reporting the declining health of the wife of one of Arizona's leading cattlemen, Mr Bruce Gentry of the Valley of the Sun.

Birch Kent did not pause to wonder how come an item of such plainly localized interest should have found its way into a New Mexican newspaper, nor how the mention of that man's name brought back memories of the Valley of the Sun and of Painted River.

His mother's health was the only thing on his mind as he prepared to ride.

Hugh Legler was brewing coffee over a campfire in a cavern above Iron Pass as Frank Wise put his horse to the steep climb. The bodyguards were taking it in turns to watch the entrance to the western end of the valley – twelve hours on and twelve off.

The Sonoran Desert region in which these two rested, was rich in both habitats and species, both animal and man. The species of man these two body-guards were, could best be termed as dangerous.

Arizona comprised the extreme south-western portion of the United States. It is bounded on the north by Nevada and Utah, on the east by New Mexico, on the south by Sonora, on the west by California and Nevada.

Each of the bodyguards had spent many of their years in Arizona, but also had been in other parts of the United States. Rumors floated about that Wise was wanted back east for the murder of his wife. No one was really sure of Legler's past and no one dared to ask.

When hatching their scheme to establish if Birch Kent was dead or alive by drawing him out of hiding, they had not foreseen the possibility that they might be called upon to put it into action. However, they understood the necessity for this, for only the two of them and the Gentry family knew that Birch Kent was the infamous outlaw Birch Hamilton, and the secret had to be kept. Big Bruce would be ruined if it ever

became known that he had fathered, albeit illegiti-
mately, a notorious outlaw.

Big Bruce Gentry had his sights set on a seat in the
senate and planned to seriously pursue this goal after
his wife had died and his power base on Alpha Ranch
was secure.

But first things first. As long as there was a possibility that his bastard son – Birch Kent – was alive, he
posed a threat on a personal and professional level.
Big Bruce could not live with that possibility. If Birch
was dead, his problem was solved. If he was not, Big
Bruce wanted him dead. And he wanted him dead
now.

Scar-faced Frank Wise had brought rum for the
coffee and they sat on a rock drinking the potent
brew and gazing out over the rain-soaked bleakness
of the pass.

'No sign,' Hugh Legler reported unnecessarily.
'And it has been at least three days since the boss
planted the item about his missus in the paper. Hell,
the joke would be on us if the bastard has been dead
all this time.'

'He could be alive, but laid up . . . you know . . .
wounded at least. Seems no doubt he was shot up in
Nevada.'

Legler massaged his shoulder. It was stiff, and the
doctor had said it might always be that way as a result
of Birch's bullet. Legler wanted Birch dead, but was
by no means certain it was going to happen here.
Gentry seemed convinced that his advertisement
would draw Birch, if he was alive, and calculated that

144

he would come in from Nevada on the western trail, hence the round-the-clock lookout at the pass.

The rock surface north of the Colorado Chiquito and Grand Colorado rivers were untainted stonework, mostly sandstone. There were portions of the Great Colorado basin where history could be traced all the way back to fierce volcanic eruptions as in various places it was covered in scoria and ash. Between the Sonora and Gila rivers there could be found numerous types of surfaces: limestone and granite being the two most prevalent.

The landscape caught the bodyguards' attention, but did not deter or distract them from their mission.

'If he is alive, he will come,' Hugh Legler said emphatically. 'Big Bruce is sure of it, and so am I.'

'Big Bruce believes it because he wants to believe it,' Frank Wise grunted, his Adam's apple bobbing as he gulped his coffee, messily. 'But just because he believes it, doesn't mean it is so. Big Bruce is a hard hater by nature, but there ain't nobody he hated like he hates his bastard son.'

Wise lifted his field glasses to his eyes to scan the sweeping landscape. Arizona was a land of marvels for those who traveled here to look for the American dream or men like them, who looked for a place to escape their pasts. Nowhere on the globe can the operations of nature be traced more clearly and distinctly. Torn and riven by stupendous gorges and deep canyons, crowned by lofty mountains, and diversified by immense plains, grassy parks, beautiful valleys, and elevated mesas, the topography of the country in variety, weird beauty, and massive grandeur, is not excelled on the continent. That the great plateau of Arizona was once an inland sea, there can be little doubt; and the isolated mountain masses, rising like islands above its surface, and the fantastically castellated buttes, which dot its immense plains.

Frank Wise continued, 'He always hated him, seems to me. But once Big Bruce got his eye on Andrea, and he caught her rollin' in the hay with Birch, that put the lid on it. Remember that night. . . .'

Hugh Legler remembered every detail without any trouble. He remembered the flogging and the pursuit, with Big Bruce threatening every hand with the sack if they did not haul Birch back, dead or alive. But most of all, he remembered James Felder going down with a bullet in the heart, shot dead by a sixteen-year-old kid with his back torn to shreds by a whip. It was one of the most impressive and chilling incidents Legler had ever witnessed in his life.

Ever since that night, Legler had been wary of Birch Kent, in absentia. Birch's return to Alpha Ranch had refreshed his memory of just how dangerous he was. He had made them all look bad. Big Bruce included. And now, because of the rancher's obsession with obtaining clear title to his kingdom, they were engaged in the business of trying to lure Birch back so they could put him six feet under the ground and make sure he stayed there.

For his part, Hugh Legler was hoping Big Bruce's

ploy would be crowned with success. He would much rather that than wait for him to return in his own good time . . . which he undoubtedly would.

Birch Kent had two powerful attractions here, his mother and Andrea Gentry. Frank Wise genuinely believed that he would return if he was still breathing, while Legler was trying to convince himself he would.

'What is that over Bald Knob?' he asked sharply, glimpsing distant movement.

Below the knob and the canyon, the Gila forms a valley from one to five miles wide, which produces luxuriant crops by irrigation. The Santa Cruz, from its source in the Huachuca mountains, after flowing southward through Sonora, making a curve to the west, and passing by Tubac and Tucson, enters the Gila by an underground channel below the Pima villages. Salt River unites with the Gila at the point of the Sierra de Estrella. It is a bold and rapid stream, having its source in the White mountains, and carrying a volume of water nearly three times as large as that of the Gila. Its upper course is through deep canyons, occasionally widening into narrow and fertile valleys. The main branch of the stream is known as Black River, flowing through a rugged, mountainous country. It receives the White Mountain, Carizo creek, Tonto creek, and other streams from the north, above the canyon, and the Rio Verde below that point. After breaking from the canyon, the Salt River runs in a south-westerly direction, through a wide plain, containing the largest body of farming land in the Territory.

Frank Wise focused the field glasses, then shook his head. 'A condor?'

Hugh Legler squinted. 'What is it doin' flapping around in the rain?'

'Must have been disturbed by somethin'. . . .' Wise remarked.

He suddenly lowered the field glasses. They exchanged glances. Disturbed by something, or someone?

'Here, give me a look through those things,' Legler growled, and snatching the field glasses, pressed them to his eyes.

It was some ten patient minutes before the watchers were rewarded, and Wise did not need the help of field glasses to spot the bobbing shape of a horse's head with a man's Stetson showing above its ears, suddenly appear over the top of the rise.

'It is him, ain't it?' Frank Wise breathed.

Hugh Legler did not answer until he was sure. 'It is him. Get the horses, Frank!'

CHAPTER 13

TROUBLE AT PAINTED RIVER

Adeline Gentry called, 'Andrea, what is going on?'

Andrea came back from the window and took the sick woman's hands in hers. 'Uncle Bruce is sending the hands and servants into town, Adeline. Don't ask me why. I do not know why.'

Adeline frowned. 'Into town? What on earth for? What is going on?'

Andrea Gentry did not know, but it was with the intention of finding out that she left the sickroom and hurried out onto the veranda in time to see the disgruntled housekeeper and two young maids climbing into the buckboard, with cowboy Montana Seger on the driver's seat.

No point in asking them, Andrea told herself.

They looked even more confused than she must have.

She went looking for her uncle, but Big Bruce was watching her from the long adobe bunkhouse which had been emptied out, except for himself and his bodyguard, Hugh Legler.

'What are we gonna do about her, boss?' Legler asked of his employer.

'You mean Miss Andrea, my niece, not "her", Hugh.' The tone was meant to teach his bodyguard some decorum, but came out as harsh.

'Sorry,' Legler grunted in response, and thought, 'He is still crazy about her, even though she treats him like a rabid dog.' Aloud he said, 'But what about Miss Andrea? She ain't gonna like what is about to go down here.'

What was going to happen, was that Birch Kent would ride into a seemingly deserted Alpha Ranch headquarters, and be cut down by Big Bruce and his bodyguards. The workers had been sent off so there were no witnesses. Birch Kent would simply vanish from the face of the earth, and if his mother did not voluntarily sign over her share of the spread to Gentry, she would be buried with her son.

Big Bruce Gentry had finished pussyfooting around. The time had come for him to deal with those who stood in the way of his ambitions.

Andrea remained a problem. Big Bruce would never hurt her, but she would hate him even more than she did now when he had killed Birch, and possibly Adeline. Thinking about this, the cattle baron decided that she, too, must be removed from Alpha Ranch while his bloody business was being conducted.

He sent Legler to find her, but the big man finally returned empty handed. Andrea was nowhere to be found, and Legler could only suppose she had gone to town with the servants and cowboys.

Big Bruce did not have time to worry about his niece. Legler and Wise had ridden in from the pass at a gallop, but even if Birch was coming in at a walk, he must show up soon.

The trio took up their positions, while Adeline Gentry lay, confused and feverish, in her big double bed, wondering at the unnatural quiet and praying for the strength to get up and find out what was going on, and why Andrea had deserted her side.

Birch Kent stopped his horse by a sycamore tree and looked down at the headquarters. He had felt tired as he covered the last five miles across Alpha Ranch's sweeping acres from the pass, but the sight of the big house spread below revived him.

Yet he dreaded what he might find here. His mother had never been strong. Had his recent visit been too much for her? His eyes strayed to the burial plot by the river. The river rose in the valley, in the great plateau that stretches south from the San Francisco mountains. It pursued a southerly direction, most of the way through a beautiful and productive valley, receiving in its course Oak, Beaver, and Clear creeks from the east, and Granite creek from the west. It joined the Salt River a few miles below Fort McDowell. The length of the Verde is nearly a hundred fifty miles. It carried a volume of water almost equal to the Gila, and is one of the finest streams in the Territory of Arizona.

What if there was a new cross there already? Birch could not get the image from his mind. How could he live with that?

He prayed he would not be too late, while at the same time taking out his pistol to check the cylinder before moving on. Birch smiled wryly; he was praying for a life while readying himself to take another. This had to be the strangest moment of his life, yet at the same time, he saw it as inevitable.

Adeline must live.

Big Bruce Gentry must die.

Nothing could be simpler than that.

Molly Floyd's face floated before his eyes as the horse carried him the final half-mile. His mouth tightened. Adeline would just have to understand why he had to kill the son of a bitch she was married to. He should have killed Gentry when he had the chance, instead of taking the whip to him.

Strange, but his back did not itch now. He felt strong and relaxed, completely healed. He felt that Big Bruce Gentry would need a squad of cavalry to keep him at bay tonight. And even that would not be enough, for although his body might be shot to hell, his hate and thirst for revenge would keep him going.

The heavy-legged horse was carrying him past the

corrals when Birch suddenly applied light pressure to the reins to bring the animal to a halt.

Alpha Ranch headquarters, bathed in the glow of the house and yard lights in the early dusk, was quieter than Birch could ever remember. Where was everybody?

Birch slid from the saddle and faded into the gloom between two sheds, while anxious, hidden eyes searched for him. Then the sudden, sharp sound of hoofbeats came from the direction of the town trail.

'Who is it?' hissed Big Bruce from his position at the tank stand. The question was directed at Legler, who was spread-eagled on the roof directly above him.

'Judas Priest!' came the whispered response from the darkness. 'It is the goddamned Marshal, Elliot!'

Rigdon it was indeed. The lawman had been at supper when Andrea arrived in town to insist he ride out to Alpha Ranch and find out what was going on. The farthest thing from the marshal's thoughts as he closed in on his objective was the possibility of the arrival of an outlaw or a bloody ambush.

But Marshal Rigdon Elliott, veteran of a hundred dangerous manhunts, would pay for not knowing, for taking Andrea's concerns a little lightly and for being preoccupied with thoughts of Adeline Gentry.

It was decision time for Big Bruce and in less time than it took to cock his rifle, he had made it. Elliott must also go. Big Bruce could not allow the lawman to foul up the scheme that had, so far, succeeded even better than he had hoped.

The rifle roared and the marshal pitched from his saddle, watched by a wide-eyed Hugh Legler, an expressionless Frank Wise, and a startled Birch Kent – all from different positions in the shadows.

But as Big Bruce jacked another shell into the rifle and prepared to finish off the lawman, Birch's pistol roared to life and a hole suddenly appeared in the iron tank above the rancher's head, dousing him with the water.

Elliott crawled desperately to the meat house as Big Bruce's roar filled the night. 'Finish the badge-toter first, then get the bastard! He is in the feed shed!'

The alacrity with which Legler and Wise leapt to do Gentry's bidding was due partly to obedience, but mostly to self-preservation. A Federal lawman had been shot. If they did not finish him, they could end up stretching a rope. It did not take the veteran hard cases long to figure that one out.

Elliott was in bad shape. Hot lead was snarling about him and two fast-shooting ruffians were closing on the flimsy meat house from opposite sides, when Birch appeared. He toted two six guns and was shooting from the hip.

Helpless, bleeding but totally aware, Elliott watched the gunfight with wide eyes. He saw Birch stop a bullet, then Wise crashed into the corral fence and fell on his back.

'Get down, Birch!' Elliott heard himself shout, but he was the only one who did. Birch certainly did not as he went for the other bodyguard – Legler – behind buckling guns. He was creased again, but that did not stop him. And now Legler, wounded himself, but refusing to back down, came rushing from cover, guns blasting, and walking into a leaden wall of death that knocked him to the ground in a bloody heap.

Birch's guns were empty when Big Bruce appeared at last, emerging from the shadows by the tank stand, coiled whip over one shoulder and the rifle in his powerful hands.

And he was smiling broadly.

'I should have done this the day you were born, but it is never too late,' Big Bruce spoke as he approached Birch. 'So long, bastard!'

On his knees in the dirt, useless pistols dangling from his big hands and regret welling up inside him, Birch had only one consolation for what was happening now:

He would die a man, not the scared boy he had been long ago when this hatred began.

It was not much of a summary for a life, but it was still better than nothing, and his lips were framing a silent farewell to the two women he loved when the gun roared.

Birch had closed his eyes and waited for the impact that did not come. Instead, Big Bruce Gentry – his father – took two uncertain steps towards him, staggered, then turned slowly as a ghostly figure appeared on the gallery.

It was his mother – Adeline – and she held a smoking rifle.

'You!' Big Bruce croaked. 'You double-crossin' bitch!'

Birch was struggling to rise as Big Bruce raised the rifle he held. He shouted to his mother to back up, but his words fell on deaf ears. Adeline was not retreating. She would do what she must, what she felt she should have done long ago.

Big Bruce's rifle was within an inch of firing level when Adeline fired her rifle again and blew a hole through the heart of her husband – Big Bruce Gentry.

Waiting was the hardest part; waiting to see if the townspeople would accept their story; waiting for the verdict of the sheriff; even waiting to see if Marshal Rigdon Elliott might suffer a change of heart and throw Birch Kent into prison again, instead of referring to him as 'Birch Hamilton' and insisting that he had played a heroic role in the trouble at Painted River or the terrible affair at Alpha Ranch.

The trouble or affair, as related by the wounded marshal, had been an attempted takeover of the ranch by two gunmen-bodyguards with ideas above their station, resulting in their violent deaths and the death too, regrettably, of the Valley of the Sun's most eminent citizen, Big Bruce Gentry.

The story was entirely the veteran lawman's creation and idea. He had concocted it in the first flush of relief and gratitude towards Birch Kent after having his life saved during the ranch house ambush. And although Birch and Elliott had been lifetime friends, Birch was not sure that later, the marshal's sense of honesty might not force him to retract his story and divulge the truth which would, of course, provide Birch with a one-way ticket back to Yuma Territorial Prison.

But Adeline, who was well on the way to recovery since her husband's death, insisted that Rigdon Elliott, who had never regarded Birch as a true outlaw, was not taking his daring stand just to express his gratitude, but also as a means of casting aside the iron strictures of a lawman's way of life in favor of doing what was right, rather than what might be strictly legal.

And Adeline Gentry was finally proved to be correct when the circuit judge announced the case closed, and the valley was free to applaud its newest and, perhaps, most unlikely, hero, Birch Kent.

There were lights in this mother's eyes and color in her cheeks again. And Andrea? Andrea was radiant and looked several years younger as they sat around the supper table with the marshal carving the joint and Birch pouring the wine.

They were celebrating the doctor's verdict that Adeline now showed every sign of a full return to good health, which the doctor attributed mainly to the power of prayer. They all agreed and thanked the Lord daily for her return to health.

But watching his mother and the lawman Elliott clink glasses and drink, Birch knew different. Adeline was doing better health-wise simply because the dragon was dead and her lifelong savior had been proved, his love for her beyond all doubt.

The new will and deeds lay on the table. Alpha Ranch now officially belonged to Birch Kent, which was a matter of towering importance to his mother but of very little significance to her son, Birch.

Unlike his mother, Birch had never dreamed he might one day inherit his father's land. All he had ever wanted was a peaceful, happy life. And now, if the gods were good and if, living here with the three people who meant the most to him in the world, he might go through life never being identified as the notorious outlaw Birch Hamilton, he would be happier and richer than he had ever dreamed possible.

It was a gamble for them all, but then, all life was a gamble, Birch mused. And looking into Andrea's stunning emerald eyes, he knew this was one gamble he was destined to win.

The house that his father – Big Bruce Gentry – had ruled with such hate, rang with the sounds of laughter, merriment, music and happiness as the moon looked down on the Valley of the Sun.